SILVER
WOLVES

JEROME CHARYN

SILVER WOLVES

a novel

SEVEN STORIES PRESS
New York / Oakland / London

Copyright © 2026 by Jerome Charyn

All rights reserved.
No part of this book may be reproduced,
stored in a retrieval system, or transmitted in any form,
by any means, including mechanical, electronic,
photocopying, recording, or otherwise,
without the prior written
permission of the publisher.

SEVEN STORIES PRESS
140 Watts Street
New York, NY 10013
www.sevenstories.com

LIBRARY OF CONGRESS CATALOGING-IN-PUBLICATION DATA

Names: Charyn, Jerome author
Title: Silver Wolves : a novel / Jerome Charyn.
Description: New York : Seven Stories Press, [2026] | Audience: Ages 12-17
Audience: Grades 7-9
Identifiers: LCCN 2025005568 (print) | LCCN 2025005569 (ebook) | ISBN 9781644215180 hardcover | ISBN 9781644215197 ebook
Subjects: CYAC: Conduct of life--Fiction | Gangs--Fiction | Interpersonal relations--Fiction | LCGFT: Novels
Classification: LCC PZ7.1.C49518 Si 2026 (print) | LCC PZ7.1.C49518 (ebook)
LC record available at https://lccn.loc.gov/2025005568
LC ebook record available at https://lccn.loc.gov/2025005569

College professors and high school and middle school teachers
may order free examination copies of Seven Stories Press titles.
Visit https://www.sevenstories.com/pg/resources-academics
or email academic@sevenstories.com.

Printed in the United States of America

9 8 7 6 5 4 3 2 1

In memory of my own big brother,
Harvey Charyn, former Homicide Detective First Grade, NYPD,
without whom I could never have conceived this book.

And for all my friends at the High School of Music and Art:
Jerry Schneider, Margie Biancolli, Billy Dee Williams,
Marcia Glassmer, the late Fay Levine, Levi Laub, Liselotte Fellner,
the late Ed Kleban, the late Sue Levitt Stamberg, Carole Lewis,
the late Peter Yarrow, Henry Kellerman, the late Harry Hurwitz,
Robin Allen, the late Jane Wagner, Sheldon Clare,
and my lost sweetheart, Anita "Vicki" Karp

Contents

I
PORTRAIT OF THE ARTIST

ONE
Spofford ◆ 3

TWO
Hermann Ridder ◆ 21

THREE
Castle Billy ◆ 27

FOUR
The Polish Rider ◆ 35

FIVE
With The Messengers ◆ 43

SIX
The Star Boarder ◆ 53

SEVEN
Creedmoor ◆ 63

EIGHT
The Bashful Prince ◆ 73

NINE
The Belevedere ◆ 81

TEN
The Storyteller ◆ 91

ELEVEN
Overtone ◆ 101

TWELVE
The Missing Sapphire ◆ 111

II
LOST AND FOUND

THIRTEEN
Broken Bones ◆ 125

FOURTEEN
Merriman & Merle ◆ 135

FIFTEEN
War ◆ 141

SIXTEEN
Boundaries ◆ 157

SEVENTEEN
A Sunday Girl ◆ 169

EIGHTEEN
Anita ◆ 183

NINETEEN
At the Figaro ◆ 193

TWENTY
King of the Crag ◆ 203

TWENTY-ONE
Cannibals ◆ 213

TWENTY-TWO
Yellow Eyes ◆ 223

TWENTY-THREE
The Tall Package ◆ 235

I
PORTRAIT OF THE ARTIST

ONE

Spofford

GREYNESS, ALL GREY.

The walls, the windows, the sky, the roaches, the rats, the guards' batons, the matrons' matted hair. A sea of grey on dry land. That's what Spofford was like. The Bronx's own juvenile jail. And I had to laugh, even if my jaw was swollen from the bashings I got. Spofford was run by New York City's Department of Juvenile Justice. But the only justice I ever saw at Spofford was a kick in the can.

Every delinquent was supposed to have a savior. Mine was Mr. Milbank. He visited once a month from Juvenile Justice. He had a walrus mustache, Mr. Milbank. He looked ancient to a kid of fifteen, with a forest of hair in his nostrils. But he couldn't have been older than forty. He had a brown vest, a brown suit that stank of mothballs, brown socks, and brown sandals. It was a relief from all the grey.

Milbank wasn't unkind. But he didn't have much of a wallop in a detention center where all the bosses were brigands and thieves, including the warden. They stole from us, they beat us up, and when one of the guards hit me too hard, I bit his hand. My reward was the "hole" for two weeks, solitary confinement in a box made for animals to crawl on their knees. But I didn't tattle to Milbank or I would have been rewarded with another visit to the hole.

"How are you, Salt?" he asked.

My name was Jonah Salt. But Mr. Juvenile Justice never called me by my given name. I was Salt, always Salt.

"I'm fine, Mr. Milbank. I could field a baseball team with all the fleas in my prisoner's pajamas."

He looked at me with horror in his liquid eyes. "You're not a prisoner, Salt. You're in protective custody. This correction center will keep you from committing more crimes."

It was just my luck that a truant officer caught me with stolen merchandise. Me and Martin Peck, another member of our gang, the Silver Wolves, had broken into the basement of Miller's sporting goods store on Boston Road. It wasn't a burglary. It was revenge. Miller had his annual sale with a Willie Mays glove advertised for ten bucks. I wanted that glove. I was nuts about Willie ever since I saw him on the tube in '51, when he'd left the Birmingham Black Barons to play centerfield for the New York Giants. There had never been a centerfielder like Mays, at least not in my life as a baseball fanatic. He could cover the entire turf of the Polo Grounds, the Giants' stadium on the far side of the Harlem River. I'd been through the turnstiles on several occasions. It wasn't that hard to sneak in. I watched Willie lope across the grass, catch a fly ball behind his back or pluck it off the strings of his shoes.

And I wanted a glove with his signature engraved on it. But the moment I walked into Miller's store wearing a Silver Wolves jersey, he took *my* Willie Mays out of the display window and said the sale was off. He didn't like the Silver

Wolves, called us hooligans, though we kept other gangs from smashing his windows. We would always be outlaws to him no matter what we did.

I hadn't gone to school in a month. What was the point? I had to hold the Wolves together. The gang was without a general. And the truant officer happened to bump into me while I was in possession of Willie's glove with the price tag still on it. And he caught Martin Peck with a couple of Louisville Sluggers. The cops arrived and took Martin away to the precinct. Martin was seventeen and a candidate for Rikers Island, the biggest penal colony in the world. But I was too young for Rikers. That's why I was sent to Spofford, a holding pen for juveniles under sixteen. Kids were known to get lost in the system for years and end up with a grey beard before they were let out into the sunless streets. But I had my champion, Mr. Milbank.

He looked at the sketches I had tacked on the walls of my cell. The matrons always removed them and kept my art for themselves. But I had a box of Crayolas, a sketch pad, and a supply of thumb tacks that I hid under the sink.

"Quite the artist," Milbank said, scribbling in his notebook. "Our own little Picasso."

"Who's that?"

"The master of masters," Milbank said. "He lives in France, in a chateau. Whenever he fills that chateau with paintings, he locks the door, and moves on to another. Each chateau is priceless, because of the paintings." Milbank scratched his ear. "You're a savage, Salt. Haven't you ever been to a museum?"

"No."

"Then how do you learn, how do you decide what to draw?"

I didn't really know. I drew whatever appeared inside my head—each image would come in a flash, like a lightning bolt in my brain, and I would have to get that image onto my pad before it went away

"Young man, you have a wall of wolves."

Milbank wouldn't understand. I was drawing the creature that inspired our gang, the wounded wolf that wandered onto Longfellow Avenue in the middle of the night with blood on its paws, its coat covered in filth, its yellow eyes looking at us with kinship, as if me and my brother were also wild animals. We'd heard the wolf howling. That's why we went downstairs in our pajamas and bare feet. I was just a kid—maybe five and Michael was maybe eleven. "Wait here," Michael said. "And don't frighten the wolf." My brother went back upstairs in his bare feet. I didn't know what to do. I was riveted to the wolf's yellow eyes. Michael returned with some kosher salami, a container of cottage cheese, an open can of chicken soup, a pail of hot soapy water, and a washcloth.

He fed the wolf first. The wolf gobbled the salami out of Michael's hand, dug its snout into the container of cottage cheese, and lapped the chicken soup with its long pink tongue. Then Michael wiped the blood from the wolf's paws with a wet handkerchief, and bathed both paws in mercurochrome from our medicine chest. He walked around the wolf after that with the washcloth and scrubbed its entire coat. The wolf never flinched once as Michael scrubbed for half an hour, until the pail of soapy water turned black with clots of dried blood and grime.

I witnessed a miracle right on Longfellow Avenue, in the middle of the night.

All the wolf's greyness was gone. Its coat was streaked with silvery fur. I didn't know much about anatomy, but I was certain that we had found a rare wolf. I'd seen the grey wolves and the brown-coated timber wolves at the Bronx Zoo, but never a silver wolf. It must have come from a forest in Connecticut. It had battled with a wild buck, I suppose, or another wolf, crossed the Bronx River, and landed all alone on Longfellow Avenue. The wolf stared at Michael with its yellow eyes, pawed my brother once, and loped back into the dark, its silver coat shining like a silent song.

A week later, Michael met with friends of his to start the Silver Wolves, with me as the gang's mascot. My first drawing tumbled out of a dream. I wasn't duplicating what I saw, a wounded wolf coming out of nowhere. The form of that wolf flashed inside my head. That's what I drew, with a pencil. I hadn't mastered the art of crayons yet. But I told none of this to Milbank.

"And how is that criminal brother of yours?" he asked.

"Michael's not a criminal," I said.

My brother was the only general the Silver Wolves would ever have, and he was always getting into trouble with the cops. The captain of the 48th precinct advised Michael to enlist, or the cops would keep hounding him until he ended up on Rikers Island. Michael was ready to take on the entire precinct, but he would have destroyed the Silver Wolves in a rumble like that. So he signed up and served in Alaska, driving heavy-duty trucks on thousand mile runs. But he disabled his commanding officer in a drunken brawl at a bar in Anchorage, and was now at Castle Williams military prison on Governors Island, serving twenty years. Michael couldn't keep out of trouble. He scrapped with all the prison guards—years were added to his sentence. I knew that he would never leave "Castle Billy" alive.

I couldn't visit Michael while I was sitting in my cell. Governors Island was only 800 yards off the edge of lower Manhattan. I could see half the island and the circular fortifications of Castle Billy from the ferry slip. It was a ten minute ride to the island on the South Street Ferry, but it was an unpleasant ride because there were military policeman patrolling the upper and lower decks with pistols and pump guns. And I never saw one of them smile.

Mr. Milbank kept hitting a single target. "Michael Salt is the only reason you are at Spofford. His gang has brought you here. Will you resign from the Silver Wolves? I can build a stronger case for you at Juvenile Justice."

I knew I would be with the Wolves for life. I might not wear the gang's colors if I ever reached forty, but I wouldn't wear a brown vest and brown socks, like Mr. Milbank.

"May I?" he asked, and he removed a drawing from the wall of the wolf's yellow eyes. "I'll keep it as a souvenir and show it to my colleagues at Juvenile Justice. It will build a stronger case for an early release from protective custody. Don't lose your courage, Salt. I'm on your side."

Mr. Milbank was fiddling. But he wasn't much of a fiddler. I was in the system now and I'd never get free of it. That police captain was right. Michael would be sitting in Rikers if he hadn't joined the Armed Services. But it wasn't much of a trade-off. He was at Castle Billy. And he'd never leave that island fort and ride the ferry into Manhattan.

OUR CELL DOORS were rarely locked. No one had ever escaped from Spofford. The main building was surrounded by rolls of razor wire, the windows were barred, and the front and rear doors were built with armor plate. Alvin James, a lieutenant of the Boston Road Black Barons, visited my cell with a hatbox. The Wolves had never had any rumbles with the Barons. They had their territory and we had ours. His eyes were swollen. The guards must have hassled him for pocket money. None of us in custody could get a candy bar without some loose change.

Alvin was awaiting a court appearance. He was accused of stealing groceries for his sisters and his mother, who was going blind. His father was a sign painter. He'd fallen off a ladder and was in the hospital. And here was Alvin James in my cell with a hatbox.

"Open it, little brother," he said.

I removed the cover. A Willie Mays glove was sitting inside. Alvin watched my eyes pop with wonder, and he smiled.

"Take out the glove, juvie. I know you have the hots for the Say Hey Kid. He shouldn't have quit the Birmingham Barons."

"But Willie's in the majors now," I said.

"The Birmingham Barons have their own major leagues. Willie was their star attraction.

You don't know a thing about Black baseball. We had our own stars until the rich white clubs raided our leagues and ripped the heart out of whatever baseball we have left."

"But I couldn't have gone down to Birmingham to watch Willie."

"Well," Alvin said, "Willie would have come up here with the Birmingham Barons and beat the tar out of the Giants. But I'm glad I got you that glove. I know it's why you're at

Spofford. Stealing a glove and getting caught. So I got you another one."

It was a puzzle. "How did you manage that?"

Alvin laughed and ruffled his head with pride. "We're the Boston Road Barons, juvie. We have our own warehouse. And we must have a dozen Willie Mays gloves. I borrowed one. I have the receipt. But that ain't the problem. How are you gonna hold onto your Willie? Henshaw will grab it the first chance he gets."

Henshaw was in charge of our cellblock. He was an ex-hockey player. He'd been with the New York Rangers for a season as a utility man who had been knocked around and had to quit. Both his eyebrows had been scarred from the blades of opposing teams' hockey sticks. One of his eyes was in peril. He wore an eye patch. But that didn't stop him from getting promoted at Spofford. Henshaw was an assistant warden. He was also an anteater. He could scoop up whatever piece of property you had in your cell.

Alvin oiled my glove with a tiny tube of linseed oil.

"You don't want the leather to crack," he said. He handed the glove to me, and I kept digging into its pocket with my fist. He could smuggle in a glove, but there wasn't a baseball to be found at Spofford. Baseballs were on the warden's weapon list. There were only spaldeens in the sports chest. And those pink rubber balls disappeared after a day. Henshaw did organize punchball games on the roof, which was covered over with a razor-sharp net. Alvin played sometimes. I never did. I loved punchball, but not on that roof. The netting made me feel even more like a prisoner in Henshaw's prison.

Alvin stayed with me for half an hour while I deepened the pocket of the glove with my fist. We never talked about our gangs or the colors we wore on the street. We were rivals, but not at Spofford, where those of us inside had to band together to survive. The loners didn't last. They grew very sad, stopped talking, and were taken to Creedmoor, the city's own psych ward. Some even killed themselves. That's why there was always a suicide watch at Spofford. Henshaw didn't want a stain on his résumé.

There was a good reason why Alvin gifted me with that glove. Michael did some research while he was at Castle Billy. He met with the military prison's eye doctor. He talked about the eye disease Alvin's mother had: glaucoma. He was able to locate special eye drops that would slow down his mother's blindness. He had the Army eye doctor write out a prescription and I delivered it to our local pharmacist, Mr. Swann. The eye drops cost over a hundred dollars, but Michael paid for it. And the Barons and the Wolves had a temporary truce, so I could hand over the eye drops to a Baron in Baron territory. Alvin was in Spofford at the time.

We didn't talk about the eye drops or the favor Michael did. But that's why there was no other general like my brother, even if he was behind bars. He knew the landscape, the entire terrain. And Michael had magic in his hands. He'd created his own silver wolf with soap and water. He was aware of the needs of his rivals and enemies.

Alvin took my oiled glove and returned it to the hatbox.

"Alvin, where will you hide it?"

He laughed. "With Matron Millie's other hatboxes. She has twenty of them stacked outside her office." Millie was our nurse. But she administered punishment as well as bandages and balms. She was the weightlifting champion of the East Coast who had nearly made the Olympic team. When she wasn't in the infirmary she was in the gymnasium, doing squats with a mountain of weights on her shoulders. When she got mad, she would wander across the facility and toss aside any of us who were in her way. If there was a riot in the cafeteria, she would arrive, and the riot ended right there. I didn't fear Millie, though she had cuffed me enough. I just felt sorry for her. I could tell how lonely she was.

But Alvin's hatbox trick didn't work. Millie rummaged through her hatboxes and discovered my glove. She looked at all our records, and realized I had been remanded here for stealing a Willie Mays glove. I was summoned to Henshaw's office. I watched all the hockey scars ripple across the side of his face without the eye patch. Millie was there, sitting on the edge of his desk.

"Jonah," she said with a softness that had a hint of violence. "My poor little
Jonah. All you had to do was ask me for a Willie Mays. I could have gotten that glove for you. Tell me, son, who sneaked it into the facility?"

She snorted at my silence. One of the other matrons brought in Alvin James. He had cotton balls in his nose to stop the bleeding. The guards must have punched him silly. He wobbled on his feet like the drunken sailors I had noticed on the South Street Ferry.

"Now who will be the first to confess?" she asked with a chuckle. Millie was having a great time. She would escort us into the latrine, strip us, strap each of us to a chair, and hose us down until our lungs were ready to burst. The telephone rang before Millie could drag us to the latrine.

Henshaw picked up the phone with a growl. But he

turned into a sweetheart the moment he recognized the voice at the other end of the line.

"Yes, Cap. . . . Sure, Cap. No harm will come to the kid, I swear."

Henshaw handed me the phone. "Dummy, the Cap wants to talk to you."

I put the receiver to my ear. "Hello?" I squawked like a mouse.

"Jonah, it's Captain Lawrence. How are they treating you, kid? Have you spoken to your brother? And don't worry about the glove."

I was curious and a little pissed. How the hell did Captain Sheldon Lawrence of the 48th precinct on Bathgate Avenue hear about the baseball glove that Alvin James had smuggled into Spofford in return for some precious eye drops? I had to be cunning with the captain. I had to be shrewd.

"I haven't seen Michael in months, Cap. I talk to him whenever I can. But we don't have too many phone privileges."

"I'll take care of that. Give me back to the hard-ass."

I returned the phone to Henshaw. I could hear the captain scream. Henshaw's hand

shook. He put the phone back in its cradle. His good eye was on fire. But he dismissed Alvin and me.

"Here," Millie said, and tossed me the Willie Mays.

I HAD MY baseball glove. I should have been content, but that encounter in Henshaw's office troubled me. Without Michael, I was the last thinker the Silver Wolves had left. As Michael would say if a situation or a particular detail bothered him—"Something stinks." Who had told Captain Shelly Lawrence about my Willie Mays? And how did he happen to call a couple of minutes before Alvin and I would have landed in the latrine to get hosed down?

Captain Shelly must have had his own snitch at Spofford—he had snitches everywhere—and that snitch must have told him about the trouble Alvin and I were in. And it was just our luck that the captain happened to phone Henshaw in time to save us from Millie's water treatment . . .

It was visitors' day, but I seldom got the call to come downstairs. Michael was at Castle Billy. Mom had to work two shifts at the chocolate factory on Southern Boulevard, and Pop was imprisoned in his armchair. He'd been the best auto mechanic in the Bronx, with his own repair shop, but his partner stole from him, his own nephew robbed him blind, and when the shop closed, Pop fell apart. He grew mean. Michael had to stop him from slapping me around. Pop sat in his armchair all day staring at the wall, or watching whatever program was on the tube. Michael said he was a candidate for Creedmoor. Mom said he had once been the handsomest man she had ever seen, like a movie star in a garage mechanic's coveralls. He was a terrific kisser when he courted her. And she wouldn't give him away to any psych center. That's why she had to work two shifts. But suddenly, I could hear my own name crackle on the loudspeaker.

"Jonah Salt, Jonah Salt, to the common area. You have a guest."

I wondered if it was a trap, if Henshaw wanted to kidnap me and hide my bones in another institution. It made no sense. I went down to the common area, where the visitors came. What guest would have traveled to Hunts Point, at the eastern edge of the Bronx, to have a look at me? I got my ticket from the matron in charge and went into the visitor's room. Mom was waiting for me. She must have come between shifts at the chocolate factory. She looked pale, but everyone stared at her. Not even Pop's surliness as he sat in his chair could wash her beauty away. Nothing could. I realized for the first time that her lavender eyes had a touch of yellow that was as riveting as Michael's silver wolf. Her neck was long and lean like the swans in Crotona Park. Her body swayed with its own rhythm. Broken as she was by Pop's decline and her endless hours at the factory, she still seemed to move with defiance and grace.

Both her sons were in jail and she managed to smile.

"Anita," I said. That was her name. I never called her Mom. "How did you get here?"

"I took a cab, juvie. You're worth it. I'm worried about your brother. He doesn't write. He doesn't call."

"They must have put him in solitary," I said.

"Will you call him, Jonah? For my sake."

She began to sob in the visitor's room. I wiped her eyes with one of the laundered handkerchiefs she sent me through the mail.

"He doesn't want me to visit," Mom said. "He says it makes him sad to see me at Castle Billy."

"Anita," I said. "You know Michael. He's a sensitive soul."

"So sensitive," Mom said with that actress's flair she had.

She looked at me with her punishing smile. "So sensitive that he nearly broke his commander's back. Jonah, I'll go mad if you have Michael's violent streak."

She'd brought me a roll of nickels from the bank, a fresh supply of handkerchiefs, and a pecan pie she'd made after midnight.

She stared at my Willie Mays. I couldn't leave it in the cell. It wouldn't have been there when I got back.

"Where'd you get that? Isn't it the same glove you took from Miller's window?"

"No, Anita," I said. "It's another Willie Mays."

I could tell that everyone in the room was jealous of me. Nobody had a mom like mine. She gave that wretched room the only glamour it would ever have.

I DID HAVE a court date. It was on the calendar. And I was assigned a lawyer from Juvenile Justice. I never met with him, not once. A week after my encounter with Henshaw, I was summoned to his office a second time. He had a scowl on his face. His eye patch quivered.

"Mr. Salt. You're free to go. All charges have been dropped."

I knew that Captain Shelly Lawrence had arranged things. The captain was an arranger. He had clout at Juvenile Justice and with most of the judges at Family Court. I was free to go with my bundle of unwashed clothes and my Willie Mays.

I walked home from the facility. I'd forgotten to collect my keys. We lived on Minford Place now, near the elevated tracks. When the train rumbled past, the windows rattled and the crockery shivered on the shelves. And no matter how inventive Mom was, with nails and hooks in the walls, a cup would shatter once a week from the vibrations.

I rang the bell. When Pop didn't come, I banged on the door. I waited ten minutes
before Pop came and undid the locks. He didn't believe in hugs. He whacked me on the side of the head. He was weak now. I could have fended off that blow. I didn't. It probably gave him satisfaction, made him feel alive, to whack his son.

"Why did you knock so loud?" he grumbled. Spittle ran from his mouth. "And where'd you get that baseball glove. Did you steal it?"

"No, Pop. It was a gift from another gang."

"Gangs," he said. "Always gangs."

Pop's mind was working. I could tell. His right ear twitched whenever he was deep in contemplation. Pop realized that pretty soon he wouldn't be able to whack me. I was getting too big. And I lifted weights. I did curls and bench presses in the gym at Spofford. And we had barbells and dumbbells at our headquarters in the abandoned building across the street, on Minford Place. There'd been a fire in the building several years ago. The landlord collected his insurance and ran. The city couldn't find any suitors. No other landlord wanted to purchase the property. So the fire-scarred building sat there. And Michael claimed it as our clubhouse.

My biceps measured fifteen and a half inches. I could have clobbered Pop now that he was wasting away in his chair. But I loved him in spite of the beatings. It was Michael who had protected me, who took the blows in my place when I was a little boy.

Pop had once been a handsome man. The handsomest ever, according to Mom. And he always wore a greasy shirt from the garage. That didn't matter to Mom. Now he sat in soiled pajamas, with blackened toenails. Pop could fix any car before he had his accident. If the rear axle didn't align, or the battery was dead, or the radiator was busted, or the tailpipe farted, Pop could fix it. Then the car jack collapsed while Pop was crouched under the chassis of a Ford convertible, and his bones were crushed; he lay in agony for months at Lincoln hospital. He was never the same after he returned home in a hospital gown, hopping from room to room on crutches. I'm not sure what the nurses had given Pop to kill the pain. But now he sat in his chair with a grizzled look, a grey man.

Pop never served in the military during World War II because he was deaf in one ear. But he did have "an essential occupation" as a mechanic at the Brooklyn Navy Yard. Sometimes he slept in the barracks on Navy Street, Mom said. I was a little kid at the time. And when he returned home wearing a borrowed sailor's cap and pea coat, every woman in the neighborhood, married or not, was jealous of "Anita's sailor."

No one was jealous of him now. He had that unfocused glaze in his eye.

"Your brother's in solitary again," Pop cackled. "You can't visit Michael. Castle Billy won't let you in."

"Pop, how do you know?"

"They called from the Castle," Pop said with a demonic look. "Your big brother is locked up. He's lost his visiting rights."

Pop nearly tripped, and I had to help him back to his chair. He was so frail, I could see his chicken chest under his robe. I'm not sure why, but I kissed his forehead.

"Stop that," he said. "You're a convict out on parole."

I went into the kitchen to make a turkey sandwich. I was starving. But I lost my appetite after one bite. I went downstairs to the gang's headquarters with my Willie Mays. I walked right into that abandoned building across the street. I wondered now why the cops never bothered us, never tossed us out on our asses, or why the Fire Department never appeared. It was an account of Captain Shelly Lawrence.

The bricks were crumbling. You could sniff the rotting earth rise up from the cellar. We occupied the ground floor. But I didn't find the semblance of a gang. I found a few of the Wolves making out with their girlfriends—the "debs" or "debutantes." Michael called them *Wolverines*. He liked that word. The Wolverines wore our colors. Our jackets and jerseys were unique to the Silver Wolves, thanks to Michael. I drew a pair of piercing yellow eyes on tracing paper, and the gang's own tailor, Wallenstein, made a pattern out of it and stitched it onto the back of every jacket. Wallenstein was also our fence. He paid us for every bit of merchandise we "collected." His tailor shop was right on Southern Boulevard.

I was disgusted with what I saw in our clubhouse. We were a gang with an absent general. And I was the general's kid brother with a baseball glove. I couldn't wake up the Wolves.

I did miss one of the Wolverines. Her name was Wendy— Wendy Weg. She was my sweetheart until she moved out to Long Island with all the other Wegs. Her pop was a grocer and he had a string of groceries in the South Bronx. He didn't want Wendy to be a Wolverine. Michael was worse than Al Capone in his imagination. And it killed Mr. Weg to watch his favorite daughter going steady with Al Capone's little brother. He wouldn't allow me to pick her up at his luxury apartment on Crotona Park East. It was the only block in the neighborhood that had buildings with doormen. And if I went near the building, Mr. Weg's doorman would say, "Sorry, kid. The grocer hates your guts."

I saw Wendy on weekdays at school. But we couldn't make out in the halls. There were monitors on every floor. So we had to get together at the clubhouse, where we didn't have to kiss in secret. And then the Wegs moved away. Wendy promised to write. But all I ever got was a single postcard with one crappy sentence and a cryptic goodbye:

Jonah, keep away.
Wendy, forever yours.

So I was wistful about Wendy, wistful about the Wolves.
I went back out onto the street. I almost wished I was at Spofford again and couldn't witness the decay of our gang.

TWO

Hermann Ridder

I HAD TO go back to school. I was in the eighth grade at Hermann Ridder Junior High. Ridder was the first junior high built in the Bronx devoted exclusively to the seventh, eighth, and ninth grades. It was famous for its SP (Special Progress) classes, where the smartest kids could skip a grade. The biggest brains from all over the Bronx went to Ridder. You could see them in the halls. They hung out together and had contempt for anyone who wasn't in the SPs. Ridder was a twentieth-century castle. It took up an entire square block between Boston Road and Crotona Park and was made of glistening white stone. It had a façade that was shaped like a shield.

I wasn't in the SPs. I was a renegade. I'd been left back and lost a year. That's why I was surprised when Mrs. Martingale, the guidance counselor, pulled me out of class on my first day back at Ridder and had a monitor accompany me to her office. Martingale was the one who wouldn't let me advance to the ninth grade and forced me to mark time. So I figured she would scold me and say that I would be left back another year.

But Mrs. Martingale smiled and her pursed lips revealed a tidbit of warmth. "You're a rascal, aren't you, Jonah Salt? Your brother was a rascal, but he was never left back. Michael, isn't that his name?"

"Yes, Ma'am."

"And where is he now?" she asked with the same pursed lips.

"In solitary confinement at Castle Billy—on Governors Island."

She was getting curious. "And what is Castle Billy?"

"A military prison, Ma'am."

I'd misjudged Mrs. Martingale. She seemed concerned about my brother. "How long will he have to stay at Castle Billy?"

"For the rest of his life, Ma'am."

"What a pity," she said. "Your brother was so bright. But I have a plan for you, Jonah. Have you heard of the High School of Music and Art?"

"No, Ma'am."

"Well, it's a special high school for young artists and musicians with excellent grades. But the dean informed me that the school has a dire shortage of male students. Do you have a portfolio, samples of your work that you might take with you for an *audition* at the school?"

"I do have a portfolio. But I don't understand. My grades stink."

She was annoyed with me now. "Haven't you listened, Jonah? The school is desperate for males with talent. Music and Art might overlook your miserable academic performance. I've seen your art, young man. You do have a gift. Don't disappoint me. I've scheduled the audition—or test, or whatever they call it. It's for next week."

I stood there. "But what if I don't want to take the test? What if I want to stay at Ridder?"

All that coldness I remembered had returned. Her face tightened. "Jonah Salt, you have no future here."

MUSIC AND ART was another castle, a much older one than Hermann Ridder, with gargoyles that looked like fearless goblins that sat on their haunches and could spit fire. The school was on Convent Avenue, in Harlem Heights. I had my portfolio. I'd been drawing and doing sketches ever since that wounded wolf visited us on Longfellow Avenue. We'd moved to Minford Place after Pop's accident. The apartment was smaller and the rent was cheaper. And Minford Place was within walking distance to the chocolate factory where Mom worked her two shifts.

I no longer had the Bronx River as my inspiration. I knew that we'd never hear a howling wolf on Minford Place. It was too far from the river and the river's wet soil. Nothing lived on the concrete except roaches and rats. I rode the train into Manhattan and arrived at Music and Art. Ushers showed me up to the third floor. I entered an art studio that was filled with girls and two lone male troopers like me. The art teacher was a woman in her forties with streaks of silver hair. We all sat around a large table as the teacher went from portfolio to portfolio. She stopped at mine, glanced at my sketches, one by one, paused and smiled.

"Jonah," she said, looking at my name tag, "you seem to have an infinite passion for wolves."

"Yes, Miss Wellman." That was the name on her tag.

She ran her finger across one of the sketches. "You have such a delicate line. But I would have expected a little more variety. You must love the wolves you draw. Every detail is so exact."

I didn't tell her about the wounded wolf. I just nodded my head. And then Miss Wellman sat down, with her hands on her knees, and said, "Well, my illustrious young artists, now it's time to get to work. You all have a supply of sharpened Number 2 pencils in front of you, with a gum eraser and a sketch pad. You have twenty minutes to capture me as best you can."

Several of the girls raised their hands. They seemed in a panic. They wanted a few more details about this assignment, Music and Art's entrance exam. But Wellman took out her stop watch, pressed a button and said, "Tick-tock. Please don't waste one second."

I had an advantage: the silver streaks in her hair. I drew Miss Wellman as a wolf without yellow eyes. I gave her a full chin rather than a snout. I marked the bottom of my sketch—*Jonah Salt, Hermann Ridder Junior High*—and returned it to Miss Wellman. She seemed less interested in us after all the sketches were handed in. She had a new batch of students waiting for the entrance exam.

I wasn't worried. I'd caught the silver in her hair with my Number 2. I didn't need the gum eraser. Two weeks after the exam, a notice arrived in our mailbox on Minford Place. It was a form letter with my name penciled in. I'd been accepted at M & A.

A monitor brought me into Mrs. Martingale's office at Hermann Ridder. She waved her own letter that she had received from that special high school. "Aren't you proud of yourself? We had three applicants, and you're the only one who got in."

I was curious. "Were the other two boys or girls?"

Martingale glared at me. "Girls, of course. Both were in the SPs. And you, the straggler, got into M & A. Isn't that a tale, Jonah? The Dean wrote me. She said your work was highly original. Something about wolves. Now don't disappoint me. If you fail your courses, you won't get in. And I couldn't tolerate a misfit like you for another year, the only boy at Hermann Ridder who graduated from a correctional facility."

"I didn't graduate, Ma'am. They kicked me out."

And she laughed. I'd bet it was the first time in her life. "Even Spofford didn't want you. Behave, Jonah, you hear?"

I BEHAVED.

Hermann Ridder was just like another prison, but without cockroaches. I suffered from what is now known as dyslexia. It was hard for me to read a page, any page. I had to shape every word in my head, sound out a sentence, syllable by syllable. But I realized that my school career was over if I was left back again. I'd never get into Music and Art. And I liked that castle with the gargoyles that could spit fire.

So I read and read. Sometimes it helped if I touched a word on a page, pretended to shape it with my hand as I pronounced each syllable. I kept up with the class. I couldn't revive the Wolves while Michael was in solitary, and I had no reason to cross that channel from South Street to Governors Island. I needed Michael's hand, Michael's brains. And I needed luck. So I went everywhere with my Willie Mays.

I had to depend on Mom for pocket money. Sometimes I did favors for Wallenstein, the gang's tailor, whose store was in the shadow of the elevated tracks on Southern Boulevard.

I did sketches for Wallenstein. Michael called the tailor a very refined man. Wallenstein had come from London after World War II. He'd been the personal tailor to duchesses and dukes, but Michael thought that Wallenstein had something to hide, that he was running from the shadow of a crime. He must have been sixty. We drank Earl Grey tea together with digestive biscuits, which were impossible to find on American shelves. The biscuits had little holes punched in them and were made with malt and wheat flour.

I drew portraits of his best customers for him. I also made deliveries. He would give me bundles of cash, which he called "bricks," and I would deliver them downtown to a shifty trader on Gold Street. I suspect the trader was stockpiling Wallenstein's cash and investing it in risky stocks and bonds that paid a very high interest. But there was no record of the trade. Often, on these journeys, I would walk from Gold Street to the South Street ferry and visit my brother. But I couldn't do that now.

Wallenstein saw how wistful I was.

"Not to worry, Jonah. Michael's the clever one. They'll have to let him out of the dungeon at Castle Billy. You'll see him again, very soon. Have another biscuit, lad."

And we sat there, the digestive biscuits crumbling in our mouths with their half-sweet flavor, as the Bronx El train passed over our heads. His sewing machine rattled, his spools of thread tumbled all over the place, and the lights blinked and went out. I didn't give a damn about the dark. I had my Willie Mays.

THREE

Castle Billy

THE WIND WAS pulling hard while I was on the ferry. The waves washed across the lower deck, and the attendants, who wore billed caps, told us to climb the crooked stairs to the upper deck. I climbed with the wind at my tail. The ferry was a wreck. The captain's cabin had bite marks in it and white pellets of bird crap on its slanted roof from the seagulls that hovered over the ferry. The military policemen wore helmets and spats. They put down their pump guns and wiped their shoes and spats with a wet rag. They watched me with suspicion, saw the wolf's yellow eyes on the back of my jacket ripple in the wind. It couldn't have comforted them, staring into yellow eyes that were meant to be sinister and to dishearten rival gangs. It was Michael's idea to have me sketch the wolf on tracing paper for Wallenstein. Only a general could have thought of the chill an image like that would bring. Michael was like a chess master, moving imaginary pieces on an imaginary board, always ten leaps ahead. The gang was an empty nutshell without him, lazy and worthless.

We arrived at the ferry slip on Governors Island with a

slight bump. Most of us on the ferry hadn't come to explore Governors Island. We were either the friends or relatives or sweethearts of people imprisoned at Castle Billy. Michael had lots of sweethearts. They followed him around everywhere before he went to Alaska and arrived at Castle Billy in shackles. They never visited him on this forlorn island. Their moms and pops wouldn't allow them near a military prisoner, the outlaw of Castle Billy.

Our own mom had so little time, working as she did sixteen hours six days a week. But on Sundays she cooked Michael's favorite candy—peanut brittle—for him, hopping around the stove with a carton of brown sugar and a jar of Planters roasted peanuts. I loved to watch her break the sheet of caramelized candy into chunks of brittle and pack those chunks into the Planters jar. That's what I brought with me to Castle Billy.

It could make you heartsick. That circular fort of faded red sandstone stood there like a monument without pity. It had holes in its walls for cannons that used to protect the harbor. The holes looked like empty eye sockets. I didn't have an easy time. The only ID I had was my student subway and bus pass. The guards were curious about Mom's jar of peanut brittle. They spilled out the peanut brittle onto a rubber mat and broke the brittle with their filthy fingers. Then they returned the pieces to the jar, licking the crumbs that were left.

I had to store my wallet and keys in a cubbyhole and sign a statement that Castle Billy was not responsible for any lost or stolen valuables. I had little choice. I signed. Then I waited on a bench, while others who were on the same ferry ride were accompanied into the visitors' room. I ended up the last person sitting there. I looked at the Timex I wore on my wrist. I was a half hour away from the last ferry back to South Street.

Finally a guard brought me into the visitors' room. It was empty except for Michael, who sat at a far table, his ankles chained to a table leg, so that if he wanted to run from Castle Billy, he'd have had to drag that table everywhere he went. He was gaunt, my big brother, who once had the biceps and the build of Mr. America. We'd worked out together at the clubhouse on Minford Place.

I started to cry. Castle Billy had broken my brother. Half his teeth were missing. His whisper sounded like a whistle because of the empty spaces in his mouth.

"Don't cry in here," he said. "Not in front of the guards. And why'd you wear our colors at Castle Billy?"

"I forgot. I was so glad that you called and . . ."

He glanced at the peanut brittle.

"The guards touched every piece," I said.

I could tell how disappointed he was. "Then leave it for the rats on this island."

"Brother, you kept Pop from beating me a hundred times, and I can't even smuggle in some peanut brittle."

"Ah, kid," Michael said, "I hate that you have to skip a day of school."

"Michael, I got into Music and Art. It's thanks to you. If you hadn't washed down that wolf on Longfellow Avenue, I'd never have seen her silver streaks. And I would have had nothing to draw."

Suddenly he was our general again. "Those drawings are sacred. They belong to the Silver Wolves."

"I had to put a portfolio together," I told him. And I shifted into another subject with all the deftness of a Silver Wolf. "Mom worked so hard on the peanut brittle."

"And Pop?"

"He sits in his chair and looks at the walls."

Michael removed a crumpled sheet of paper from the pocket of his prison uniform—all grey. "I wrote Pop a letter. I worry about him. Mom's strong. She'll survive. But Pop will never be the same."

We both heard the foghorn from the ferry. It was the first and final call of the ferry's last ride of the day to South Street.

"Kid, you'd better go. I'm glad that you got into M & A. Did you know that I applied?"

I was stunned. Michael had never talked about it. "You applied and didn't get in? With your grades? Weren't you in the SPs, Michael?"

"I still didn't get in. They weren't impressed with my portfolio," Michael said. "I guess I didn't have a silver wolf on my mind. Go!"

I couldn't even hug my own brother at Castle Billy. No touching was allowed.

"Goodbye, Mikey. I'll visit next week."

The guards all had a malignant grin. They knew I wouldn't make the four o'clock ferry. And I'd have to grovel on the island all night until the morning ferry arrived. I ran towards the ferry slip. I looked at my Timex. It was a quarter past four. But the ferry hadn't left the slip. The captain stood outside his cabin in a cap and pea coat. He waved. He must have recognized that I was missing. I climbed aboard and saluted him. And the ferry left with a screeching sound that was like the desperate cry of a wounded animal.

I DIDN'T TELL Mom about the discarded peanut brittle. She'd worked so hard to give Michael the one bit of pleasure he could still have at Castle Billy. I delivered my brother's letter to Pop. He dug it into the pocket of his pajamas. It stayed there. I imagined he slept with the letter in his pocket, went to the toilet with it. Then a week later, he took out the letter and said, "Son, I can't read. My sight is poor. Read your brother's letter to me."

My dyslexia was still there. I had to sculpt Michael's syllables, forge them into a melody that I could master:

To Lorenzo Salt from his Older Son

Dear Pop,
I will never see you again. I know that. We have had battle royales, regular fist fights. And I'm ashamed to say that I hit my own father, but I had to protect Jonah from your drunken fits. Please forgive me, Pop. I should have been more judicious. I could have kept Jonah out of your reach. But I must have inherited some of your wrath. I remember how loving you were before Jonah was born, how you took me to Bronx Park, carried me on your shoulders, as we marveled at the lions and their mates. You were much happier then. I know that a conniving nephew of yours stole from you, broke your heart, and you lost your garage because of him. You might not have had your accident if that misfortune never occurred. I only wish that some of your happiness remained.
Your Loving Son,

Michael Salt

Pop grabbed the armrests of his chair as I read the letter, syllable after syllable. I didn't stumble once on a word. I was shaken. I'm sure Pop was, too, though his face didn't reveal a thing. He had the same blank expression, like a man with all his feelings ripped away. But he did have feelings. His knuckles turned white and bloodless as he clung to the chair. And I realized that my own birth had complicated things for Pop. Maybe he didn't have much room in his heart for another child. I was the interloper, the second son.

Sad as I was, I could coast at Hermann Ridder now that I'd been granted entrance into M & A. But I had to be shrewd enough not to fail a subject. I struggled the most in my English class. We were reading *Johnny Tremain*, a novel about an apprentice silversmith around the time of the Revolutionary War. Out of spite, a fellow apprentice sees to it that molten silver from a cracked crucible spills onto Johnny's hand, making it impossible for him to work as a silversmith. That's what haunted the story. Johnny's hurt hand. He was just my age. But all those words on a page overwhelmed me. And at times I would lose the thread of the story and have to pick it up again. But I conquered *Johnny Tremain*. I tasted the words, felt their fabric on my tongue. I passed English and all my other subjects with a grade high enough to propel me out of Hermann Ridder.

I worked for Wallenstein during the summer. I delivered "bricks" to Gold Street. I drew portraits of half his clients. But I felt like Johnny Tremain, with molten silver poured over me. I was lost without Michael. I appeared at Castle Billy without my mother's peanut brittle. The guards must have been disappointed. They couldn't lick the crumbs off their filthy fingers.

I was the last one let into the visitors' room. My brother sat there in his shackles, his seventeen inch biceps long gone. He was all shrunken. He looked like a skeleton covered with slabs of flesh.

"Mikey, don't they feed you in this place?"

"Never mind," he said. "How are the Wolves? Do they patrol the neighborhood? We don't want other gangs invading our territory. We'll never get them out."

"The Wolves are lazy. They spend their time with the Wolverines. But I work for Wallenstein."

His chains rattled. He would have liked to knock me across the room. "Wallenstein can't hold the gang together. He does us favors. You have to rise up, kid. We'll lose the clubhouse, the entire building, if we stop patrolling the streets. Jonah, you have to be the general now."

"Pop liked your letter," I said, trying to steer him onto another subject, a trick I learned from my big brother.

Michael seemed bewildered. "What letter?"

"About the lions at the zoo."

My brother's face went as blank as an emery board. He looked like Pop in his chair.

"Kid, I can't remember writing any letter. That's what Castle Billy does to your brain."

I heard the foghorn from the ferry. I couldn't even hug my own brother. I had to race to the ferry slip again, as the guards laughed at my predicament.

The captain remembered me and waited. He wouldn't allow the military cops to bully him.

"Full consignment," the captain said. "All on board that's meant to be."

The seagulls squealed, as the ferry left the pier with a groan.

FOUR

The Polish Rider

I WORE MY muscle T-shirt the first day of class. No one seemed impressed. Not the teachers, not the girls, not the boys, who had button-down shirts, charcoal grey slacks, and white buckskin shoes, or white bucks. They were dressing like Ivy Leaguers. I had to learn what the Ivy League was, and how important it remained in the scheme of things. All the boys in the freshmen class were already dreaming of a slot at Harvard, Yale, or Princeton. I'd never heard of these schools. I knew about Spofford, Castle Billy, Hermann Ridder, and Al Capone. I'd been rescued by a silver wolf, who had catapulted me into the High School of Music and Art.

The boys wore their hair very short—a crew cut it was called. It was named after members of the crew—the rowing team at Harvard in their "shells" on the Charles River. I couldn't bring myself to have my hair shaved so short. The Wolves would have laughed at me. So I went to the Wolves' own barbershop on Boston Road and had the new barber clip around my ears and shave the back of my head. That's as far as I would go in the direction of a crew cut. I stopped wearing muscle T-shirts at M & A. I had to blend in a little if I wanted the girls to notice me. So I bought a button-down shirt at the haberdasher near Hermann Ridder and a pair of charcoal greys. That was my school uniform. I never wore it at the clubhouse. And I couldn't bear buckskin shoes. So I kept my sneakers and my moccasins.

The first assignment we had in my art class was to go to a museum and report on a painting. Our art teacher was Miss Wellman, who had looked at my portfolio and administered the entrance exam. She gave us three choices: the Museum of Modern Art, the Metropolitan Museum, and the Frick Collection. I chose the Frick, because the word "collection" seemed mysterious to me. The Frick was in a mansion on the Upper East Side. The mansion had once belonged to a millionaire who owned half of Pennsylvania and all its coal mines. I had a school pass. But it didn't matter. There was no entrance fee, thanks to the generosity of Mr. Frick. The museum contained the remnants of his private "collection."

Beside the entrance, there was a waterfall housed in a gigantic marble tub that was like a wet garden with flowers and tiny trees. Miss Wellman had warned me not to take my sketch pad and my Number 2s. The guards, she said, might get suspicious and worry that I had come to mark up and disfigure priceless paintings. But I did see kids from other schools with sketchpads and pieces of charcoal. They must have had special permission from the ghost of Mr. Frick.

The sound of the waterfall followed me everywhere like a soft, soothing caress. I stopped in front of a painting called *The Polish Rider*, and it was by a man called Rembrandt van

Rijn. The guy in the painting—the Polish Rider—looked exactly like Michael before Castle Billy made him into a ruin. He had Michael's high cheekbones, Michael's dark eyes, and Michael's fearlessness and pluck. The Polish Rider was on a white horse. He was looking to one side, indifferent to my gaze. He was a warrior who carried a quiver of arrows and an armory of other weapons; in his right hand was some kind of hatchet, clutched in a fist that curled outward in defiance as he sat on his battle horse.

I bonded with him right away. The Polish Rider could have been one of the Silver Wolves from another century, come to visit the South Bronx in his orange pants and orange crown.

I didn't want to let go of the Rider, even if I couldn't capture his gaze. It was like having Michael again in my midst. Then I twisted to the left and saw a self-portrait of the painter himself, Rembrandt van Rijn, as an old man. He sat in the shadows, wearing a red sash. His face was blotchy; he was decked in furs. But he had none of the Rider's brashness or allure. All his scarves couldn't hide the gentleness of his nature. An old man without any illusions, no matter what finery he wore. Rembrandt van Rijn peered right at me. Our gazes met, and our eyes locked for a moment. I called him Uncle van Rijn, even though I couldn't pronounce that name.

We all had reports to write about the experience we had in our different museums. I was the only one who had chosen the Frick. I was the outsider. The others talked about Picasso as if he was a relative of theirs. I had never heard of *Les Demoiselles d'Avignon* and other masterpieces of his. They worshipped his art, and they knew more about

Rembrandt—his models, his poverty, his old age—than I could have ever learned from one outing at the Frick.

It didn't matter that I wore button-down shirts. I wasn't like them. I didn't dream of getting into Harvard and "making it for life." I was a member of the Wolves, even if I went to the Frick. And it was obvious that I didn't have the gifts or the ambitions of these Music and Arters. I was ostracized, mocked, because I couldn't read very fast. But I did have one function: I was the protector of the freshman class. When upperclassmen bullied a freshman in the halls of the school, or on the front steps, or near the lockers, or on a subway platform, I served as his champion.

Mark Manheim, a senior, stopped me in the boys' locker room with his friends around him. They were all wearing the school's colors—burgundy and light blue—as members of the basketball team. Mark considered himself the lord and master of M & A. His father had graduated from Harvard and Mark was destined to follow him there. M & A was an academic school perched at the top of Harlem Heights. Art and music mattered, but were more like decorative skills to the very best students, who coveted their academic averages. Mark was sure to be the graduating class's valedictorian—the senior with the highest grades. He was also captain of the basketball team, its star center. Manheim was six feet five. He meant to blow on my chest and have me disappear.

"Salt," he said, "I'm told you've been a little too fancy with your fists. Are you going to rescue every freshman? It's our prerogative as upperclassmen to rule as we see fit. Is that understood?"

"No," I said.

Manheim was much too much in love with himself to look directly at me.

"Shall I put you out of commission, Salt?" he asked. "Shall I pull down your britches and break your ass?"

"You could certainly try."

I had baffled the big brained basketball whizz. Now he did have a look and he must have seen a silver wolf with clandestine yellow eyes. Suddenly he was out of moves. But he was in front of his friends and half the freshman class. So he pretended to box with me, and moved about with a lot of swagger. It was a big bluff. I grabbed his fists in midair and squeezed as hard as I could. I'd been using hand grips at the clubhouse. He crumpled to the floor in his burgundy and blue.

I let go of his fists and walked out of the locker room.

NOW I WAS feared, but I still had no friends at M & A. And I still had trouble in my English class. My teacher, Mr. Merriman, was chairman of the English Department. He asked me to read aloud a passage from *A Tale of Two Cities*, a novel about the French Revolution, where everyone, good and bad, had his head lopped off by a sinister contraption known as the guillotine. The book was written by Charles Dickens, who, according to Mr. Merriman, had worked in the basement of a boot-blacking factory when he was twelve, scrubbing ink bottles into the night; he never got over the trauma of that event and the belittling of his self-esteem. The passage I read was by a character in the book called Sidney Carton, a British "barrister"—a lawyer who argued cases before a judge and had to wear a wig and a black gown in court. Carton also suffered from low self-esteem and considered his life a failure. In the novel he goes to the guillotine in place of another man and gives the following speech. I had trouble pronouncing the words. I faltered. "It is a far b-b-better . . ."

Merle Messenger, the brightest student in the class, picked up where I left off in a seamless way.

"—thing I do than I have ever done; it is a far better rest that I go to than I have ever known."

The other students in the class were all jealous of Merle, because she knew the answer to every question and was such a whip. They mocked her behind her back. I was troubled by how cruel and spiteful they were, how they volleyed slurs against her. They feared her intelligence, her willingness to grapple with every problem. Like Michael, she was a born adventurer, prepared for any quest.

She'd contracted polio as a child and had a twisted leg. She couldn't walk without a cane. And it was this cane that the other students rebelled against. It was retractable, like a telescope. And the art students would draw pictures of Merle and her retractable cane. She was an outlaw at M & A, just like I was. But we were lucky to have Mr. Merriman. He valued Merle's gifts, and he wasn't bothered by my dyslexia. I wrote a composition for his class about *The Polish Rider*. I described the Rider's arrogance, how self-assured he was in his saddle. I had Michael in mind, and said how a warrior general had to take chances, and had to be fearless, or he would fall.

Mr. Merriman put three check marks at the top of my composition, to show how much he liked it. He read my composition to the class and asked me how I thought Rembrandt felt about his Rider.

I was witless for a moment. And then the words came to me like lightning in a bottle.

"Sir, I think Rembrandt admired the Polish Rider and was also afraid of his ferocious side. Rembrandt was a painter, a dreamer, and saw some of the same fierceness in himself."

I didn't falter once. I didn't stutter. I didn't stop. It was like a miracle.

"I agree," Merriman said. "Rembrandt was painting a dream portrait of himself. He could unmask his own savagery."

Merle raised her hand. "It wasn't a dream portrait, sir. It was a wish. Rembrandt was painting what he wanted and could never be."

FIVE

With the Messengers

She had a doe's big brown eyes. And I'd developed a crush on Merle. She wasn't like the Wolverines, who wandered across the clubhouse as they mourned Michael's absence. One of them, Diana, had her eye on me. I suppose she was the only one who didn't see me just as Michael's baby brother. But I was already a world apart from Minford Place. And Diana went on to become the sweetheart of another member of the Wolves.

Merle's mind was like a fortress full of melodies. And I loved every one. But Diana caught me drifting.

"Jonah, you think too much. Your head will fall off."

Maybe it would. But one afternoon, Merle tugged at my sleeve while we were coming out of class.

"Jonah, would you like to study together?" she asked in that somber voice of hers. We were having a test on *Hamlet* in our English class.

"When?" I blurted.

"Tonight," she said. "And don't bother about dinner. I'll prepare some snacks and

Mother will fix us something. You won't starve."

I took the subway home to the South Bronx. Mom was at the chocolate factory, dipping caramelized cherries into swirls of chocolate while she wore a sanitary mask and gloves and had to breathe in bits of cocoa right through the mask. I couldn't wear the Wolves' colors to Merle's. The Messengers might have been suspicious about a pair of yellow eyes. So I borrowed one of Michael's navy blue jackets. I'd filled out since he started wearing shackles, and I fit into the wardrobe he left behind when he was stationed in Alaska. I wore Michael's clothes like a twin wolf.

I rode the Seventh Avenue Line down to 72nd Street and Broadway. It was a land of apartment-hotels, where wealthy bachelors must have lived—shoe salesmen, haberdashers, skilled garage mechanics, like Pop had once been. Along the route to Central Park West there were delicatessens and bakeries where the bachelors probably gathered for breakfast and dinner and had their evening coffee and cake. This route didn't have the randomness and chaos of the South Bronx, or that stink of poverty.

The apartment-hotels all had marquees that shone like silver. And the hotels themselves had fancy names: the Winslow, the Sheldrake, the Blue Swan. But I couldn't imagine living there with all those bachelors. Then I realized that I was a bachelor myself.

Central Park West had a different complexion. It had apartment houses that sometimes took up an entire block, reached over thirty stories, had balconies and twin towers, and were made of stone.

Merle lived at the Majestic, on the corner of 72nd and Central Park West. It seemed to have six side entrances. I went to the main one. The doorman had a grey uniform. I introduced myself and asked for the Messengers. He called upstairs on an intercom that looked like several lines of bullet holes. I was escorted into the lobby that seemed as large as an ocean liner. An entire army could have camped out on the sofas. I could see my ghostly self in the waxed marble floor. The elevator man, also dressed in grey, drove me up to the fourteenth floor. A woman who I assumed was a maid met us in the hallway and led me into the apartment. I was surprised, because she flirted with me.

"Oh, you're the handsome boy with biceps and big ears from Merle's class. If she isn't careful, Jonah, I'll steal you away. My name is Flora. And if Merle gets bored with you, I can guarantee that I won't."

I didn't know what to tell Flora. I shook her hand and said, "That's a deal."

Flora seemed satisfied. She led me down a winding hallway to Merle's room. She rapped on the door twice, as if it was a signal. "Merle, your fiancé is here."

Flora opened the door partway and I had to squeeze in. Merle's room was as large as our apartment on Minford Place. She had a bed like Martha Washington's at Mount Vernon, with four posters and enormous pillows. She had her own private bathroom and a walk-in closet that I had only seen in the movies. She had a mahogany desk and a chair that was as intricate as a throne. And she had a plush black leather couch. Merle was wearing her school outfit: a sheepskin sweater, a blouse, and a skirt. She pecked me on the mouth and turned away, hiding her embarrassment.

"I'm very brazen," she said, "much too brazen."

I'm not sure why, but I wasn't embarrassed at all.

"Well, if you aren't certain about me, I might run away with Flora."

She laughed. "Don't mind Flora. She's part of the family. My father sort of adopted her. She used to be my nanny. But we have to get to work. Mother serves dinner promptly at nine. And Father can't abide it if we're late. He'll like you. He was born in the Bronx. You're borough mates. He was once very poor. He went to City College—mostly at night. And he graduated summa cum laude. That's means with highest honors."

"I know that," I said. It was a lie. "And what does he do now—for a living?"

"*Bricolage*," Merle said.

"What does that mean?"

"Oh, this and that," Merle said. "Father's a speech writer for President Eisenhower. He also has his own advertising agency. He served under Ike during the war. He wrote all of the Allied Commander's communiqués. And now Ike won't deliver a speech until Father has gone through every word. We get calls from the White House every day. I shouldn't tell you this. It's a big secret. But Father's calls are patched through to the Oval Office."

"Patched through?"

"Oh," Merle said, clucking her tongue. "He doesn't have to deal with the White House operator. But we have to talk about Hamlet's ghost. Isn't that our assignment? To figure out if the ghost is Hamlet's invention or really exists?"

"Couldn't he be both?" I asked. "Real and unreal?"

"Oh," Merle said. "That's the easy way out. Either Hamlet summons him, or the ghost summons himself."

"But none of Hamlet's friends ever hear the ghost speak."

Merle shook her head in denial. "And why would the ghost speak to them, pray tell? And what does the ghost reveal? That his own brother, Claudius, seduced the queen, and while the king is having a nap in his orchard, Claudius sneaks up behind him and pours a vial of poison into the 'porches' of his ears, seizes the throne *and* the queen, Prince Hamlet's mother. And what is the ghost's constant refrain to the prince?"

I hadn't forgotten, as hard as it was to unravel the words of the play. "*Remember me, remember me.*"

"Exactly," Merle said. "And what does Prince Hamlet do for most of the play?"

"Procrastinate."

Merle prodded me with her cane. "Worse. He prances about for two whole acts. A killer without purpose. He stabs an old man, kills two courtiers, maddens his sweetheart until she drowns, has a duel, and finally, finally, after his mother drinks poison meant for him, he brings himself to stab the king. . ."

"Merle, you're much too harsh. The prince kills when he has to kill."

"You speak like a lawyer—no, a negotiator, who negotiates every step Hamlet takes."

Just then Flora knocked at the door. "Time for dinner, *mes enfants*. Your father will be furious if you're not at the table in five minutes."

"Nonsense," Merle said. "Let him wait."

She walked to the bathroom and washed up, spraying her underarms with perfume and adjusting her bra, right in front of me.

"Your turn," she said.

I went into the bathroom. Merle or the maid had set out a fresh towel for me. I liked the rounded pieces of tile on the floor, faucets shaped like steering wheels, a shower curtain with Paul Klee's pirate ship painted on it—see, I was beginning to swallow bits and pieces of knowledge. I admired Klee's demonic ship captain, with his white and pink flags that represented the fierce autonomy of art, beholden to nothing and no one. Michael could have been that pirate. But he'd never gotten into Music and Art.

MERLE'S FATHER HAD grown up on Charlotte Street, a few blocks from Minford Place. He'd gone to P.S. 61, just as I did. But Hermann Ridder hadn't been built yet. There was no such thing as a junior high in his day. He went directly from P.S. 61 to James Monroe High School, across the Bronx River. He played on the varsity basketball team. His grades were poor. He worked in the garment district. He was drafted during World War II. Serving under Eisenhower changed his life.

He married a girl from New Hampshire, Alice Frye. She was slightly taller than her husband and had blue eyes. We sat at a big round table in a dining room that overlooked Central Park. I could see across the vast expanse of the park to the apartment house castles on Fifth Avenue. I could see the Reservoir in the park that looked like a mammoth blue-green liquid dime. Flora didn't serve us. She sat at the table, smoking a cigarette. It was Alice who served the meal, Alice who maneuvered from the stove to plate after plate. Mrs. Messenger—Alice—seemed to have magical hands. She would sit with us for a second and then return to the stove, while Merle's father—David—sat in his king's chair. I learned that he had been a corporal in General Eisenhower's entourage. He caught the Supreme Allied Commander struggling over a speech, and the corporal took out his pencil and changed a few words. Eisenhower smiled, and from that moment Corporal David Messenger followed the general right through the war. He rose to the rank of captain. But he was a modest man. I had to tease this story out of Flora and Merle.

He must have been forty years old. But he didn't look sloppy and pale, like Mr. Milbank, my "savior" from Juvenile Justice in a rumpled brown suit. David Messenger was lean and wiry. He was wearing a polo shirt to dinner. He served the salad with an enormous prong. He had two scars at the edge of his mouth—war souvenirs, I figured, but I couldn't imagine the battles he would have been in at Eisenhower's side. I was wrong. Those scars were from another war. He'd had his own gang, the Charlotte Street Rangers, and had to battle it out with other gangs that were soon forgotten, even in Bronx lore.

"Merle tells me that your brother is in solitary confinement on Governors Island."

"It's not his fault, sir," I said.

"You can call me David. We're eating salad at the same table. Is he at Castle Billy?"

"Yes—David, sir. There's nothing much else to do in Anchorage but drink beer and whiskey. And I'm not sure why, but he got into a fight with his commanding officer. Michael says he didn't start the fight. But he's a finisher, sir. I guess that's his biggest virtue and his greatest fault."

"David," Flora said, "why don't you get the boy released? You have Eisenhower's ear."

"Oh, I couldn't do that. It would be taking advantage of whatever little authority I have. And I would be involving Ike in the mess. But I still might be able to get your brother out of solitary, Jonah. Wait here."

Merle's father went into another room. He was gone for fifteen minutes. None of us took a bite of food without him. Then he returned to his king's chair. He didn't mention my brother or Castle Billy.

We had salmon and broccoli. I watched the others as they manipulated their knives and forks. I was a copycat. I'd never had dinner on Central Park West. David talked about himself. How he'd been a copywriter after the war, then had his own accounts, and then his own agency. He'd written speeches for Eisenhower, so why couldn't he write "copy" for department stores and soap manufacturers and soft drink bottlers? He never boasted about his relationship with the President to possible clients. His own modesty made him in demand.

David poured wine from a pitcher and allowed Merle and myself a sip. Otherwise we drank seltzer that was known as sparkling water on Central Park West. It was Alice who had prepared the dessert—pecan pie with a scoop of vanilla ice cream. I was delirious after the first bite. We all drank herb tea, a habit David had acquired when he was with General Eisenhower in France.

We'd been at the dinner table for two hours. I could tell from my Timex. Alice talked about her own childhood. She'd gone to a one-room schoolhouse in rural New Hampshire. Then she went off to Mount Holyoke, where she met Flora.

"Can you imagine?" Flora said. "We walked the same

grounds as Emily Dickinson." Who the hell was Emily Dickinson? I had no idea. Merle nudged me and whispered in my ear. "Amherst's queen of solitude," she said. "And a poet."

Flora and Alice had been classmates at Mount Holyoke. Alice had gone to Manhattan and married David, while Flora held several jobs and succeeded in none until she was hired as Merle's nanny. And now she didn't have much to do. Merle called her the "majordomo," head of the household staff. But she was actually Alice's live-in friend.

The two of them stood up with red wine on their lips, clutched each other like chorus girls, and recited one of Emily Dickinson's poems:

> *Success is counted sweetest*
> *By those who ne'er succeed.*
> *To comprehend a nectar*
> *Requires sorest need.*
> *Not one of all the purple Host*
> *Who took the Flag today,*
> *Can tell the definition*
> *So clear of victory*
> *As he—defeated— dying*
> *On whose forbidden ear*
> *The distant strains of triumph*
> *Burst agonized and clear!*

I didn't think of the dying soldier, or any of the purple Host, whoever they were. I didn't think of Amherst's poet queen, or of Alice and Flora, who looked like singing sisters. I thought of Michael in his jail, hearing those distant strains of triumph as he sat dying, day by day.

The telephone rang in the next room. It almost seemed like an appendage to the poem. David returned with the telephone and plugged it into the wall. He said a few words and passed the phone to me like a hot potato.

"Hello?" I said. "Who is this?"

I heard some static and then Michael's voice came through. I nearly dropped the hot potato.

"Kid," Michael said, "where are you? They let me out of solitary. Just like that. Where are you?"

"With some friends."

"You must be in the stratosphere. Who should I thank for this?"

"Mr. Messenger. He writes speeches for President Eisenhower."

"Kid," Michael said, "can you pass the phone? I'd like to thank Mr. Messenger."

"Call him David," I said and passed the phone. I didn't listen in, though Michael's voice was clear enough.

"You're welcome," David said. "We're all very fond of your brother. But I won't be able to do it again."

David hung up. I was delusional. I thought the silver wolf was sitting in the next seat.

But my cunning hadn't disappeared. Whatever they did to Michael, they had to know that President Eisenhower was on his side.

I should have been overwhelmed by David's magic trick—raiding the White House with a simple telephone call. I should have been dizzy and nauseous, but I had a ferocious appetite. I devoured my third slice of pecan pie—like a starving silver wolf might do. I was a silver wolf. I glistened under the lights of David's dining room.

SIX

The Star Boarder

MICHAEL'S HONEYMOON AT Castle Billy didn't last. Maybe Ike's own generals had gotten to Ike, because my brother was back in solitary after a week. I couldn't ask Merle's father to intervene again. He liked having me around. I must have reminded him of his own wild boyhood in the South Bronx. And after my second study date with Merle, he asked me why I couldn't sleep over? "It's a long ride back to the old neighborhood. And we have a spare bedroom. Shall I call your parents?"

"That won't be necessary, sir. I wouldn't want to intrude."

"Nonsense," he said. "We would all enjoy your company."

I went home that night. The subway cars were half empty as they crept along with that endless screech. At Simpson Street, the train was so close to the window of a seedy hotel that I could almost have reached in. It was near midnight. My mom was home. She had prepared supper, but I had already eaten. She was still wearing her factory uniform, smeared with chocolate, and the bonnet that came with it. She could tell that I wasn't hungry.

"Mom, I met this girl at school. Her name is Merle Messenger. We've been studying together, and her father suggested that I sleep over."

Mom began to brood. "Where do they live?" she asked after a long silence.

"On Central Park West."

Mom hid her face behind a paper napkin. "Lucky boy. You'll be their star boarder. Will I ever see you again?"

Mom always came home with rings of chocolate around her eyes and chocolate glue on her eyelids. She had to scrub for half an hour before bedtime to get rid of those stains and have her eyelids unglued. But I could see a tear ride down one of the chocolate rings.

"Mom," I said, "I don't have to be anybody's star boarder."

"And what do I have to offer? A cold supper at midnight and a husband who hasn't been a husband to me or a father to you since his accident? I lost your brother years ago. And now I've lost you."

I held her in my arms. I was much taller than Mom. I'd shot up like a beanstalk during my last year at Hermann Ridder. I was the tallest freshman at M & A. I was now Michael's height and I had the muscles he used to have. A weird thought stuck in my head, as if *my* growth had diminished him somehow, even if I had nothing to do with his bar fight in Anchorage and his time spent at Castle Billy. Mom was pretty tired, but I danced with her around the kitchen and hummed a waltz I'd heard coming from one of the music classes at M & A.

Mom laughed. "Jonah, you're like your big brother. You were a bandit from the day you were born."

The plates rattled in their racks. I didn't care. It was Pop who intervened from his armchair.

"Stop that racket—please." He no longer shared the same bed with Mom. Pop was glued to that chair, day and night.

"Anita," I said, "I'm nobody's boarder. I'll study with Merle. I won't even stay to have supper."

"That's rude, Jonah. If the Messengers ask you to eat with them, stay. And then excuse yourself. Being with your father is like coming home to a haunted house. It's not his fault. The accident sucked the life out of him."

It wasn't that easy. Soon I was studying with Merle every weekday. And I looked forward to my sips of wine and my conversations with all the Messengers. One Friday night we kept talking until two in the morning. Mr. Messenger wouldn't let me ride the subway that late. He went downstairs in his slippers and had the doorman hail a cab. He knew I didn't have enough money in my pocket to get me across the Madison Avenue Bridge with its braided metal roof and into the Bronx. Mr. Messenger took a silver money clip out of his pocket and gave the driver a twenty-dollar bill.

"Take care of this boy. He's precious to us."

As the driver drove off, I shouted through the window, "Please, Mr. Messenger—David—keep a tab. One day I'll pay you back."

"Jonah, you already did," he shouted, running a few steps. "You make my daughter happy."

I noticed how nimble he was as I rode into the night. I hadn't been in a cab more than once, when Mom and I went to Lincoln Hospital right after Pop's accident. I felt like a prince in the back seat, as if I owned the world.

I didn't get to Minford Place until a quarter to three. I raced up the three flights of stairs. Pop greeted me at the door. He grimaced at me and whacked me once on the shoulder. "Your mother was worried sick." I was too old now to be whacked like that. My shoulder throbbed. That blow must have cost him, too. He nearly tripped. I had to carry him in my arms like a baby back to his chair. Mom came out of the bedroom in her terrycloth robe—a gift from Michael. I'd woken her. I could tell.

"Anita, I'm so sorry."

She touched my face with her hand and went back into her bedroom.

I COULDN'T NEGOTIATE like my brother could. But I made a pact with Mom. I'd sleep over on Central Park West twice a week. She could tell how much nourishment I had from my meals and my talks with the Messengers. And she wouldn't have to think about having another outlaw son with the Silver Wolves.

Merle and I often held hands at the dinner table. The Messengers didn't seem to mind. I never actually went out on a date with Merle. But our study dates evolved into something else. We kissed and fumbled around. But most of the time we studied, studied hard. Her mind was quick, and she could read a page much faster than I could—devour it, memorize every word, while I had to *feel* a word, shape it in my mind, if I wanted to keep it. I was like a faulty juggler who missed a lot. But we acted out Shakespeare's scenes and often switched roles. Male or female didn't matter. I was Ophelia one evening and Hamlet the next.

Mr. Merriman was bewitched by us. He'd never had a

pair of students who could rip apart every line of the play. The other students began to resent us. Merle and I had read *Hamlet* out loud so often that we could break into any scene. She held her cane in the air, bowed to Mr. Merriman, and said:

> *There are more things in heaven and Earth, Horatio,*
> *Then there are dreamt of in your philosophy.*

The other kids in the class were furious at Merle and me. They were lost somehow. They couldn't memorize a single line. But they didn't have all the advantages of a study date and sips of wine. They could see the heft of my biceps and the weave of my chest under my button-down shirt. Besides, I protected them from being bullied by the seniors at school. I think they despised me as much as Merle for my mastery of Shakespeare (it was mostly Merle's doing), but I was still their savior. Merle, on the other hand, was more vulnerable. They tripped her if they could get away with it.

The leader of this cabal was Lionel Winters of Cabrini Boulevard in Washington Heights. His pop was a postman, but Lionel intended to study architecture at Yale. I had to be a general now, like my brother had always been, even if his mind was unraveling in the brig and his body had lost a lot of muscle. A threat wouldn't have worked. This wasn't the Wild West of Minford Place. It was Music and Art, where you either got on the dean's list—as Merle did—or you sat on the sidelines.

I caught up with Lionel after school. He covered his face with both hands. "If you hit me, Jonah, I'll scream. I have chronic nosebleeds. I'll have to run to the school nurse. And the dean will hear about it."

"Hold your horses. Haven't I protected you more than once—in the locker room?"

"Yes, you have," Lionel admitted gracefully. "I'm not naturally mean, you know. But it's frustrating. Merle's in another league. None of us can compete with her. And why should you care? You're not going steady with Merle."

"Suppose I am?"

He gazed at me like a wicked owl. "But she isn't wearing your pin?"

Lionel must have meant the oval lapel pin in M & A's colors that was awarded to members of Arista, the national honor society.

I was getting pissed off. "First of all, we're freshman and no freshman was ever elected to Arista. Second, the idea of pinning Merle is stupid. I don't own her."

He smirked. "Oh, but counterfeit pins are worn all the time. There's a market for them, a heavy market. Sally Grossman wears my fake Arista pin."

"I already said the pinning business is dumb. Do yourself a favor, Lionel. Don't ever trip Merle again."

I had a premonition of bad things to come when I arrived on Minford place. Pop sat in his armchair staring into a void that could have swallowed the entire universe. I warmed up the meal Mom had left for him in the stove. I set up his tray with a knife, a fork, a paper napkin, a water glass, and a bottle of seltzer. He loved to pull the plunger himself and pour the seltzer out of the siphon. But he let the seltzer sit. And his nostrils didn't stir. He wouldn't waft the aroma of the chicken breast and the baked potato in its slightly burnt jacket. I tried to feed him. But he never opened his mouth. And then he started a soliloquy, as if his words had leapt right out of *Hamlet*, a *Hamlet* of his own.

"Jonah, I knew you'd bring trouble the day you were born. I could see it in your eyes. You already had secrets."

"Pop. What secrets could I have had? I wasn't even a day old."

"You wanted to take my place at the table," he said.

"I was strapped to a highchair, Pop. I sat in diapers. Mom fed me stewed prunes."

"You were a thinker," Pop said. "You wanted to steal your mother away—you did."

"Pop, you win. I'm a wolf with yellow eyes."

And I left him there. I shouldn't have gone to Merle's. I had this premonition.

WE FOOLED AROUND a bit, but I was uncomfortable, even when we kissed. I felt like an intruder from the South Bronx in a land of marble lobbies and elevators with golden mechanical sticks. Mr. Messenger arrived late. He was in the middle of a new ad campaign. We were still eating dinner and sipping wine until well after midnight. The telephone rang. I felt a shiver along my spine. Mr. Messenger went into the other room and returned with the phone. He saw me twitch.

"Jonah, it's for you."

I held the cradle in my hand. Captain Shelly was calling. He wasn't at the precinct. He was on Minford Place.

"Captain, what's wrong?"

"Wait where you are," he said. "I'm sending a patrol car. Come downstairs in ten minutes."

He hung up and I held that dead wire in my hand. Mr. Messenger didn't ask any questions.

"David," I said, "I have to go." I pecked Merle on the cheek and put on my Music and Art blazer. Merle could read my alarm. Pouring through *Hamlet*, ripping it apart speech by speech, had not only made us attuned to the play, but to one another. It was as if I could float into Merle, and Merle could float into me and sense all the danger zones of the Wolves—other gangs in our territory, the cops on our tail.

The patrol car was downstairs, in front of the Majestic. I didn't even have to introduce myself. I climbed into the back seat, and the cop behind the wheel drove off. We arrived at Minford Place in fifteen minutes, with the siren still blaring and the patrol car's lights casting a devilish red glare over the roofs. Then the car's lights were switched off and midnight returned to Minford Place.

Pop wasn't in his armchair. Captain Shelly stood in the foyer, smoking a cigarette. He wasn't wearing his uniform with the gold band above the bill of his cap. He seemed shorter in his civvies.

"Jonah, your mother's all right. She's in the bedroom with one of our medics. A neighbor must have heard the racket and called the police. That call got to me by pure chance."

I didn't have to ask, but I asked anyway. "What happened?"

"Your father went berserk. He attacked your mom. She'll be okay. We patched her up. And it's lucky I was here. I didn't arrest your dad. I had him committed to Creedmoor for psychiatric observation. Kid, I'm sorry. It wasn't a pretty sight. He bit one of my officers. We had to muzzle him."

"Where's my mom?"

Captain Shelly escorted me into the bedroom. Mom was lying in bed while a medic applied alcohol to her swollen cheeks. The worry lines disappeared from her face the moment she saw me. She asked the medic to step out of the room.

"He's not himself, Jonah. He said we were trying to poison him and steal his money."

"What money? Anita, you're working two shifts."

"He claims the chocolate factory is a ruse, and that I run to a brothel."

I had to laugh to hide my rage. "On Southern Boulevard? They wouldn't even know what a brothel is."

She grabbed my arm. "Visit him, visit him as soon as you can. I don't want him to sit alone there, in an asylum."

"He hates me. He couldn't bear to look at me from the moment I was born. He told me so himself."

"Oh, you men," Mom said, thrusting her head back. "Michael he could tolerate. Michael was the firstborn, his heir. But you were my treasure. He's such a child. Jonah, we have to protect him from himself."

I hugged Mom and went to my room. The captain had already gone. I was suspicious of his ties to us. He'd saved me once from a beating at Spofford. He'd whisked me right out of juvenile jail before anyone could steal my baseball glove. I still had my Willie Mays. I kept jabbing my fist into the pocket of the glove. I raided Michael's closet from time to time. He had his old bee-bee gun under the bed. He had his collection of books. Michael was a reader. His favorite novel was *The Great Gatsby*. I found novels hard to read. I could wander through *Hamlet* with Merle as my guide. I couldn't have done it alone. I would have been lost after the tenth line.

I pulled out *Gatsby* from under the bed. I fell asleep after the first paragraph, with Willie Mays near my pillow. Later *Gatsby* would come back into my life. *Gatsby* was on Merriman's list.

SEVEN

Creedmoor

P**OP WASN'T ALLOWED** any visitors while he was under observation. I had to wait an entire week until Pop became a citizen of Creedmoor. It was almost like going to college, but this college had wire mesh in the halls and bars on every one of its high windows. The whole complex was a tan fortress in Queens Village, a citadel with many towers. It was both modern and medieval, with a fine lawn and tunnels that led from building to building. Creedmoor had once owned farmland where its patients could mingle with cows—the cows had turned to stone. I saw a woman with blazing white hair roam the grounds in a straitjacket with no attendant at her side. She must have been a ballet dancer at one time in her life. She leapt into the wind in tattered toe shoes, performing for an audience of one, a kid from Music and Art come to see his crazy Old Man.

I had a hard time getting into the citadel. Patients at Creedmoor and their visitors had very few rights. I went into the main entrance and was met with an overwhelming roar. There was a wave of people standing in lines so crooked that it was impossible to distinguish where one line ended and another began. Old ladies with shopping bags and men with crooked backs snuck in front of me and it was hard to fight back against such little acts of larceny—they stole my place in line. It took me an hour to arrive at the front desk, which was almost as long as Minford Place. The clerk, a woman in her fifties, who was the ruler of my own crooked line, asked me the name of the patient I had come to see.

"Lorenzo Salt," I told her.

She went through an enormous ledger that was as big as the Bible. She wet her fingers with a sponge as she flipped through the pages with incredible speed. "There are no Lorenzos here," she said, "not one."

"Then they must have booked him as Lawrence Salt."

A battery of wrinkles appeared on her brow. "Young man, we don't book our guests at Creedmoor. This is not a hotel or a police station. It's a psychiatric hospital."

She flipped through the pages again and looked suspiciously at me. "What is your relation to Lawrence Salt?"

"I'm his son," I said.

She kept peering at me. "Do you have any proof?"

I had nothing except my transportation pass. But Captain Shelly had given me a card from the Police Captains Endowment Association with a note scribbled on it:

> *Please show the bearer of this*
> *card every courtesy.*
> *—Captain Sheldon Lawrence, 48th Precinct,*
> *Bathgate Avenue, the Bronx*

The clerk seemed impressed with Captain Shelly's card. She banged down hard on a bell. A guard arrived. Suddenly I had some status at the citadel.

"Dennis, take this young gentleman to see Lawrence Salt, Ward 17, a new arrival."

I accompanied the guard to an elevator bank. We had to wait a full five minutes until we were crammed into an elevator with scratches on the walls. We got off on the ninth floor and passed through an interior courtyard without a crisp of sunlight. But even in all that grey gloom, I could see the wire mesh on the doors of the dormitories where the "citizens" at Creedmoor must have slept. But I didn't catch one human face. The guard led me to a gigantic room that was like an enclosed soccer field filled with tables and benches.

"Wait here," he said.

I sat down on one of the benches. Other guards returned to this soccer field with several women in hospital gowns, who must have had to swallow a wicked cocktail of drugs. They shuffled along like zombies with a frozen gaze, sat down across from their visitors, while their particular keeper stood beside them. The soccer field began to fill. No one shouted in here. It was as quiet as a cemetery, except when you heard an occasional laugh or cry that sent a shiver across the soccer field. That's how shrill it was.

Finally Pop arrived. His keeper must have found him at a faraway ward in another part of the citadel. He wasn't manacled or wearing a straitjacket. I couldn't tell if he was doped up or not. He started to weep. It was a soft sound, almost like a song. "Where's my boy?"

Dennis, Pop's keeper, a tall Black man with a kind face,

prodded him gently with his club. "What's wrong with you, Lorenzo? Your son's right here."

Pop gazed at me. He wasn't doped up. Creedmoor hadn't wrecked his mind. He must have been in a ward with other men who sympathized with his plight.

"This is not my boy," Pop said. "He's a house wolf. He'll tear my face off if you turn your back."

Dennis had to prod him again. "Now don't play the fool, Lorenzo. Say hello to your son. He's no house wolf. I never heard of such a thing."

Pop got up from the table and walked towards the patient's entrance. It seemed like half a mile. His keeper had to race after him. "Sorry, son. Mr. Salt might be more sociable the next time."

I didn't think there would be a next time. But Mom kept hounding me to visit him.

"Your father's all alone."

"Anita, he probably has more friends in his ward than he ever had in the Bronx."

I rode out to Queens Village again, brought Pop Michael's collection of Ernest Hemingway classics.

Pop didn't look at me once, but he fondled the worn cover of *The Sun Also Rises* and returned to the ward with his stash of books cradled in his arms.

I had nothing to offer him on my third trip to Creedmoor. He had told the chief attendant of his ward that he didn't want to see Mom, that she had betrayed him and was "a chocolate witch." Those were his words. Pop didn't mention me. I was a waif who didn't exist, a house wolf with yellow eyes. He was becoming ungovernable. They had to put him in another ward, deeper in the citadel. As the general's baby brother, I was aware of the solution. He had to see Michael one last time or he would sit in his straitjacket until he starved to death.

I couldn't go to Mr. Messenger again and ask him to intervene. He'd gotten Michael out of solitary, had called the White House, and President Eisenhower had waved a magic wand. That wand could only be waved once. The hospital tried to reach Mom. I had to take the call. Pop was having hallucinations. He bit every nurse who tried to feed him. The chief attendant on Pop's new ward wanted me to visit Creedmoor and calm Pop down.

"My father doesn't want to see me, sir. He wants my brother Michael."

"Well, that's a feast," the attendant replied. "Bring your brother."

"I can't, sir. He's in military prison on Governors Island."

I heard the attendant sigh. "Then the burden falls on you."

And so I went to see my father a fourth time. Mom had prepared a lemon cake for him as a peace offering. I waited on line. I got to that soccer field, the main visitor's hall. Pop arrived in a wheelchair. He was so gaunt, and so pale, that I could see the bones practically pierce through his skin. He wouldn't say a word to me, wouldn't ask about Mom. And then one of those miracles occurred that could only happen at Creedmoor. Michael appeared. He was manacled and accompanied by two military policemen. At their side was Captain Shelly in his uniform, with all the service ribbons and gold stars. He must have put pressure on the commandant at the castle on Governors Island, and he had the entire Police Captains Endowment Association behind him. Maybe the Police Commissioner himself intervened. I didn't like the smell of it. Michael must have had some kind of a pact with the police captain. But I was happy as hell to see Michael, even if his ankles were in chains.

And Pop cried with the wonder of it. His gauntness disappeared. He was the dapper Lorenzo Salt again, even in his lunatic asylum shirt. Pop's guard allowed him to get up and hug Michael. He rubbed Michael's face with his rough, knobby hands. And Pop did a dance in his asylum slippers.

"This is my boy," he said. I watched. It all made sense. Captain Shelly was involved with the Silver Wolves. We weren't a gang. We were an extra limb of the 48th precinct. That's why the cops left us alone and never invaded the clubhouse, or had the Fire Department condemn the abandoned building. That's why I had my Willie Mays. Captain Shelly was my benefactor.

I didn't say a word. Michael scratched my head with his knuckles, like he used to do when he was the real general of our domain. Captain Shelly had a meal delivered from one of the Creedmoor kitchens, delivered right there in that soccer field. We all ate with plastic knives and forks. We had burgers and French fries. We had corn on the cob and a tossed salad. We had slices of Mom's lemon cake and the choice of a chocolate sundae or a banana split on paper plates and coffee in plastic cups. We even had a waitress while everyone else in that huge visitors' hall watched.

It was our own "Last Supper." We weren't disciples though. We were puppets, and Captain Shelly was the chief puppeteer. Michael may have been our king, but he was a flawed one—or reckless, maybe that was the word. We sat close together on the bench, and he put his arm around me. Michael could see how upset I was. He had that gift.

"How are you, kid?"

"Surviving," I said. The military cops ate with us. Captain Shelly had invited them. And Pop moved with that gentle grace he'd had before he condemned himself to an armchair. He'd been practically mute for years, and now he was talking a mile a minute.

"My boy is here," he shouted into that sad silence of the visitors' hall.

But Michael could read into my own silence. "It's Captain Shelly, isn't it?" he whispered into my ear. I was mum.

"I was never his fink, kid. I wouldn't rat on my own gang. But we couldn't have prospered without the 48th, no gang could. Not the Boston Road Barons, not the Baldies, not the Cannibals, not the River Rats. It was mutual, kid. We helped each other patrol the streets."

We were still whispering while Captain Shelly gobbled his burger and stuffed his mouth with French fries, covered in ketchup. I watched him cram a five-dollar bill into the waitress's pocket.

"All one family, ain't we?" the captain said.

Pop began to cry. "I'm so happy. I have my boy."

I clutched Michael's hand. "You should have told me about this arrangement with the cops."

"You weren't old enough," Michael said. "But you're old enough now."

Pop began to sing a song from his time at the Brooklyn Navy Yard, about the white cliffs of Dover. I didn't have a clue where Dover was. But several other patients and visitors began to sing along with Pop. We had our own songfest.

> *There'll be blue birds over*
> *The white cliffs of Dover,*
> *Tomorrow, just you wait and see,*
> *There'll be love and laughter*
> *And peace ever after*
> *Tomorrow, just you wait and see.*

I didn't feel like singing. It must have been a song from World War II that some of the old codgers at Creedmoor could dredge up from their foggy brains. Pop ate morsel after morsel of the chocolate witch's lemon cake.

"Couldn't my boy stay with me in my ward?" Pop asked.

"That's impossible," said Captain Shelly. "I had to work my ass off to get him here. He has to go back to Governors Island."

The house wolf was half-blind. I'd never realized how totally attached Pop was to Michael. And my brother's feelings for the Old Man were just as deep. Pop clutched Michael's prison shirt. Those rough fingers of his had an iron grip. The two military cops had to grapple with him. They couldn't free my brother.

"Pop," Michael said, "I gotta go."

Pop's iron claws dropped to his side; he had a mechanic's hands, with blisters as rough and reliable as sandpaper.

"Jonah," Michael whispered before his captors led him away, "stick close to the captain. The Wolves have no future without him."

Pop was returned to his ward, and I was left behind with the captain and the waitress, who cleaned up all the debris on the table—knives, forks, and the crumbs of Mom's lemon cake.

"Kid," the captain said, "why don't you hop a ride with me?"

How could I refuse? I'd been given my marching orders from Michael himself.

We left the grounds and slid into the back seat of an unmarked car with window blinds. He pulled the blinds down, and we sat in a grey realm with splashes of sunlight. The captain had his own driver, a sergeant from the precinct.

"Kid, the party's over. Your brother can't rule the Wolves from Castle Billy. You have to deliver for him. Robberies and assaults have gone up twenty percent near Boston Road. Other gangs are occupying *your* streets. Shop owners have complained. 'Where are the Wolves?' they ask. And I have no answer."

It's true. Many of the shop owners rewarded us. But Michael never sought protection money. He never asked for a dime. We were given special favors. Michael would walk into the haberdasher near the El and walk out with an alligator belt and an Arrow shirt. But I promised the captain nothing. I was silent during most of the trip.

When we arrived on Minford place, it was the sergeant who opened the rear door.

"I'm depending on you, kid," Captain Shelly said. "Don't let me down."

I walked upstairs, went into my closet, and got out my Willie Mays. It wasn't really a gift from Alvin James of the Boston Road Barons—it was Captain Shelly who had maneuvered to get me that glove. I'd grown attached to the ridges in its pocket and to Willie's engraved signature. But it was police merchandise. And owning it felt like a crime. So I went down to the coal room, opened the furnace door, and I tossed my Willie Mays inside.

   Damn if I didn't adore that glove!

EIGHT

The Bashful Prince

Cops everywhere.

A squad from Captain Shelly's precinct raided the clubhouse and tossed the Wolves and the Wolverines out into the street. It was a kite from Captain Shelly, a message to the heir apparent—me. His men padlocked the clubhouse door. It was a major catastrophe in the life of our gang. Michael phoned me from Governors Island the next day at seven in the morning. Anita had already left for the chocolate factory—it was Mom's first shift of the day.

"Are you out of your mind, kid? Making war on the cops. Captain Shelly requested something, and you ignored that request."

"Michael," I said, "I'm not a fink."

"No one's a fink," he said. "Captain Shelly got me through the gates at Creedmoor, didn't he? Pop was practically a corpse. We revived him, thanks to the Cap. Why do you think I get special rations in here, even when I'm in solitary? I wouldn't survive Castle Billy without him. I'd be another corpse."

"Michael, what do you want me to do?"

"Go to Bathgate Avenue," he said.

"That's outside our territory. I'd get clobbered. I'll be lucky to come back to Minford Place with my pants still on."

Michael insisted. "No one will touch you, kid. They'll all know you're having a meet with Captain Shelly, or you wouldn't show yourself anywhere near Bathgate Avenue."

How could I deny my own general? I didn't disguise myself. I walked across Crotona Park in my colors. It wasn't a brazen enterprise. You had to reveal who you were in hostile terrain. This patch of land belonged to the Webster Avenue Cannibals, but the cops had a precinct in the midst of their territory, and wearing my colors signaled to the gang that I was on an official visit and wasn't trying to invade their land.

Bathgate Avenue was a Bronx bazaar, a market street with stall after stall, and people milling about, hunting for bargains, sometimes until midnight. But there were no stalls in front of the precinct. It looked like a palace in the heart of the borough, with its twin green lanterns, its tan bricks, and its massive grey stonework that surrounded a metal front door. A baron could have lived inside. Maybe he did.

I entered this police palace and approached the desk sergeant, a burly man who frowned at my colors.

"Captain Shelly, please."

The desk sergeant growled. "Is the captain expecting you, sonny boy?"

"I think so. Tell him it's Jonah Salt."

I had no trouble getting upstairs to the captain's office. It was cluttered with trophies and awards from the Captains Endowment Association and the Shomrim Society, a brotherhood of Jewish cops. There were books and baskets of papers piled on his desk.

"Well," he said, "if it isn't the bashful prince himself."

"I'm not a prince," I said.

"Would you like a beverage?"

He had a case of Pepsi Cola sitting on the floor. We both drank a Pepsi right out of the bottle. He had a bottle opener hanging from a string around his neck. The captain must have been crazy about Pepsi Cola.

"Kiddo, you have to revive the Wolves or the Webster Avenue boys will cross Crotona Park and swallow up all of your brother's territories block by block. And the Silver Wolves will become a gang of ghosts. Do you know what that means? The Cannibals will demand tribute from shopkeepers, they'll cruise around and claim all the streets."

"You could stop them," I said.

"We're not babysitters. I don't have the manpower to watch an entire gang spread its wings. The Commissioner will come down on me. His deputies will swear that Captain Shelly can't keep the South Bronx safe. And if I suffer, kiddo, Michael will suffer, too. No more trips to Creedmoor. Your Pop will waste away. They'll put him in a ward where no one will ever find him again. That's what Creedmoor is. A house of lost people. Some of the patients come with their burial clothes. They're the clever ones. They know they'll never leave that place alive."

Shelly *was* a baron, the baron of the South Bronx. But he wasn't going to rule over me. First I had to become his most valuable piece of property, and then I'd pounce. I'd studied *Hamlet* with Merle. I had taught myself to play role after role.

"You have us cornered—my brother, Pop, and me. You've even pinned my mom to that cops' clothesline you have inside your head."

"Sure," he told me. "I could get your mom fired in a snap."

"I'll bet you could."

I smiled, I nodded, and left the station with Shelly convinced I was a vassal of his. I wasn't. The bashful prince was calibrating. Captain Shelly's men had the padlock removed from our clubhouse door with a gigantic pair of pincers. And I called a meet. I was younger than the rest of the Wolves and Wolverines. And I could have had a rebellion on my hands. The Wolves weren't worried about their bashful prince, but they had lingering thoughts about pissing off Michael, even if he was an island away. My brother's presence hovered over the clubhouse like an electric string that could jolt the other Wolves at any moment.

"We have to patrol the streets," I warned, "or we'll lose our own authority over them."

"Who says so?" growled Don Barber, who was nineteen years old and captain of all the busboys at the Belevedere, a swanky cafeteria right under the El station with its mountain of stairs.

I would have been no match for Barber in any brawl. He had a stocky build and could have flung me across the clubhouse with his hairy hands. I had to use all my cunning against the busboy captain of the Belevedere.

"Think about it, Don. We won't be able to wear our colors on Minford Place or anywhere else. The Cannibals will wander across our entire terrain. They'll steal from our stores, sit on our stoops, and we'll be nothing in our own neighborhood."

Barber had grown wary of the Silver Wolves. He wasn't collecting any cash. But the gang had never been about plunder. We didn't steal. Michael hadn't started the Wolves to enrich himself and the other gang members. He'd created his own realm. If some sick old lady was starving, Michael gathered food for her from local merchants. Michael couldn't restore her health. But he could persuade Mr. Swann, the druggist on Seabury Place, to offer her cough syrup and could search for Dr. Kulack at his home-office on Charlotte Street and have him climb five flights with his medical bag to visit the old lady. Michael wasn't a glorified social worker. He was watching over his realm. There were rewards. Shopkeepers showed their gratitude. But that wasn't what motivated Michael—wealth. He was treated like a king. He solved disputes, family quarrels. Husbands didn't beat their wives on Minford place. Bullies didn't prosper around the Wolves. If a baseball glove was stolen during a game of stickball, Michael found the culprit. He went from door to door. But he had one frailty, one fault—a rotten temper he must have inherited from Lorenzo. My brother had a quick fuse. If he found a wife beater on Charlotte Street, Michael would use his fists. He could have been charged with assault, but Captain Shelly was always there. Michael would also fight with any gang member who disagreed with him. I saw him flatten the Belevedere busboy, Don Barber, several times. And Barber was his key man.

As the fights grew more frequent and Michael's temper flared, that's when Captain Shelly encouraged him to enlist. Michael was banished to Alaska, driving long-haul trucks for the military. He returned home in chains, serving out his sentence at Castle Billy. But the myth he had started, with that lone wounded wolf on Longfellow Avenue, remained. He didn't want the Silver Wolves to scatter and dissolve.

The Wolves' war council voted with me. The gang would patrol the streets and guard against any invaders. The Webster Avenue boys couldn't appear on our side of Crotona Park without some notice and without disguising their colors—light grey and blood red. Barber went along with the vote. He remained with the Wolves.

My life was more complicated now. I had to schedule all the patrols and include myself in the schedule. That didn't topple my study dates with Merle or my suppers with the Messengers. But I had fewer and fewer sleepovers. Music and Art had become a complication. I couldn't have kept up my grades without Merle. And so I resigned myself to the midnight patrols. I carried no weapons, nothing but a whistle hanging from a cord around my neck. I'm not sure what the whistle would have done. Its shrill blast, loud as it was, couldn't have woken up a single one of the Wolves. But that sudden sound would have frightened off any invaders.

Deprived of sleep as I was, I remember getting my first report card from M & A with a measure of pride. I wasn't a mediocre student, as I had been at Hermann Ridder, the boy who had been left back:

BOARD OF EDUCATION OF THE CITY OF NEW YORK
HIGH SCHOOL OF MUSIC AND ART
Convent Avenue at 135th Street, New York City

(There was a stick figure holding a palette and paint brushes in one hand and a staff with three musical notes in the other).

REPORT TO THE PARENTS OF

NAME: *Salt, Jonah*
CLASS: 1.3
ROOM: 116
OFFICIAL TEACHER: *Mrs. Ruth Rabinowitz*

And then there was the matter of my grades:

ENGLISH: 91
CIVICS: 95
FOREIGN LANGUAGE (FRENCH): 80
SCIENCE: 90

My academic average was "89." I would have clipped "90" for the first time in my life, but I had problems with French. I knew my grammar and conjugations, but the spoken word defeated me. The sounds all glided together, and I couldn't distinguish the different particles of a sentence. I was lousy on the oral exams, no matter how hard Merle coached me. The two of us were in the same class. Merle had been to Paris with Alice and David Messenger. They'd traveled there on an ocean liner, the *Ile de France*. Merle had seen all the sights—the churches, the museums, the cemeteries, and the cafés in a place called Montparnasse. where Hemingway hung out as an apprentice writer. David had his own stories. He'd been billeted in Paris as General Eisenhower's aide right after World War II. Food was scarce. But David always had his morning baguette, a long and narrow loaf of crusty bread that arrived from Ike's own French baker with a tiny tub of butter and a sliver of soft cheese.

Paris seemed like a miracle compared to Minford Place, even if it didn't have silver wolves.

"I want to live there when I grow up," I blurted out. "I want to move to Paris."

David laughed. "Look who we have here, a young Ernest Hemingway."

Alice scowled. "Don't make fun of Jonah. We'll take him with us on our next trip."

I was alarmed. I couldn't miss my midnight patrols or leave Mom alone. Alice must have understood. "Jonah can decide when he's ready."

She signed Merle's report card. Merle had a "95.5" average, the highest in the whole freshman class. No one could compete with Merle, not Armand Beglia, whose father was a physicist, or Linda Lowenstein, whose mother was a math professor. Merle was super in every subject, and that's why the most ambitious students and the least ambitious resented her. It didn't seem to matter how kind Merle was or how willing she was to help anyone who struggled in a class. They treated Merle like an outsider, and it only drew me closer to her. The second or third time we kissed (it was a very long kiss), Merle twisted a little gold chain around her finger, and said, "I guess we're engaged."

I had become part of the Messenger clan. They could see how tired I was from all my midnight patrols. As a Bronx boy himself, David understood the delicacy of my position. "A gang carries its own weight. Mine did."

"What were your colors?" I asked.

David seemed confused. Then his eyes lit under the dim lights "I remember now. . . . They were orange and blue."

I was stupefied. "Those are our colors."

"Copycat," he said.

Then I had to leave. Merle and I wouldn't fondle each other in front of the Messengers. But we kissed goodbye. The subway station was right on 72nd Street. I hurried down the steps. I wanted to be on time for my midnight patrol.

NINE

The Belevedere

It was the center of the South Bronx's little universe—not a clubhouse in an abandoned building, where rats roamed the halls, but a cafeteria under the El. *Everybody* came to the Belevedere: housewives; socialists, who were prepared to save the world over a cup of coffee; retired cops; chess players, who held tournaments at a selected table; and all the lonely people who wandered out of the cold, with the bitter screech of the El in their ears and entered into a warm blaze of light and the sound of constant chatter. Milton, the manager, met you at the door in an impeccable dinner jacket with a silk display handkerchief. If you were disheveled or tottered along with whiskey on your breath, Milton signaled to a busboy, who arrived from the counter with a bagel wrapped in tinfoil, and Milton sent you home with the compliments of the Belevedere.

I never had any trouble getting in. The Wolves at our table with their Wolverines were usually met by busboy captain Don Barber, and treated to a bowl of pretzels and celery stalks and bottles of black cherry soda by the manager. The Silver Wolves were always welcome at the Belevedere.

It was one of those cafeterias that never closed its doors, no matter what time of day or night. A rival gang would have been unwelcome. Captain Shelly wouldn't have tolerated such an intrusion. And neither would we. But I hadn't come to the Belevedere to swagger. I came to draw. I had my sketch pad and my charcoal sticks. I drew the countermen and the customers. I was a pimple compared to the young geniuses in my art classes at M & A. But I still loved to draw.

The cafeteria had its own queen. Her name was Rosalind, but we called her the Widow. Her late husband, Henry Silverstein, a mortician, had been mobbed up, as the saying goes. He happened to owe a lot of money to the loan sharks of Delancey Street and disappeared one morning. His body was never found, but Rosalind still held onto the funeral parlor across from the cafeteria. In fact, she seemed to prosper. Maybe the Widow was a loan shark herself. She always had a bodyguard with her, and she had to wake him from time to time. She drank Lipton's, which was the only tea you could find in the South Bronx. Lipton's must have had a monopoly at our cafeterias and supermarkets. I couldn't stand it—the tea tasted like dish water until I drank it at the Messengers. When I was a kid I would dunk the same tea bag into my mother's and father's and brother's cup.

But Alice Messenger always put two teabags into the same pot, and then placed a tiny knitted sweater called a tea cozy over the pot to keep it warm. The Belevedere hadn't discovered the tea cozy yet. But Rosalind did have two teabags inside her gigantic glass, which sat in a metal holder with a decorated handle and a decorated cap. This tea holder,

Milton once said, was made by Bronx artisans from a model used fifty years ago at a Russian palace in St. Petersburg.

The Widow drank her Lipton's tea and ate a slice of the Belevedere's strawberry shortcake, which sat like a tall white and red smokestack on Rosalind's plate. She must have spotted me with my sketch pad. I was wearing my burgundy and blue M & A cap. She summoned me to her table with a flip of her hand.

"Child," she said, "would you like a glass of Russian tea and a sliver of my shortcake?"

She couldn't have been much older than thirty-five, but her hair had already gone completely grey.

"Yes, I would, Widow Silverstein."

She laughed. "I'm Rosalind, please."

She snapped her fingers at Milton and had him bring a glass of Russian tea to the table and a Belevedcre dish with its blue and gold trim, together with a knife, a napkin, and a fork.

"Will that be sufficient, Madame Silverstein?"

"Yes, Milton. Now go away. I have important business to discuss with this child."

She cut me a slice of shortcake from her red and white smokestack and shoved it onto my dish. Then she stared at the burgundy and blue of my cap.

"What's your name, child?"

"Jonah Salt," I said. "And I'll be sixteen soon."

"Have a sip of tea. Be careful. The handle is hot. Did you know that I was in the first class?"

My shrug must have told her that I didn't understand what she was saying.

"At Music and Art. It was 1936. There were workmen in

the halls. The art and music studios weren't ready. We had to have our art classes in the auditorium. Some students left in the middle of the term."

"And you?" I asked.

"I stayed. And I didn't regret it. I still have friends from that first year. The workmen were gone after a few months. But that's not why I asked you over. I'd like you to do a sketch of me. I'll pay for it." She took a ten-dollar bill out of her pocketbook.

"Rosalind, I'm no Rembrandt. I'm one of the worst artists in my class. I'll do the sketch for free—if you stop calling me 'child.' I'm with the Silver Wolves."

She smiled. And the Widow from Music and Art had wonderful teeth. "Child," she said, "that's a deal. You're now Jonah, my favorite little racketeer."

I didn't contradict her. What was the use? She was the queen of the cafeteria. I took out a charcoal stick. The clarity didn't come until I thought of Michael's wounded wolf. I sketched the wolf's streaks of silver in Rosalind's grey hair. The movements of that wolf after Michael scrubbed her coat seemed to guide my hand. I had a fluidity at the Belevedere that I didn't have in my art classes, a fluidity and a freedom of design. I left Rosalind's eyes in shadow, even under the bright lights. I drew puckers of sadness under her mouth. I left the queen in mourning.

She wouldn't let me finish. That's how imperious she was. She tore the sketch out of my pad: the queen in her cafeteria, with her strawberry shortcake and her metal tea holder.

"Ah, I can see that I'm a very dour lady, Mr. Jonah Salt."

"No," I said, "you're that girl on the front steps at Music and Art. It's just twenty years later, that's all."

"Child," she said, "I wanted a drawing, not a philosophy lesson." She crumpled the ten-dollar bill, tossed it in my lap, took the drawing with her, and walked out of the Belevedere.

I DIDN'T SEE the Widow until two weeks later. She arrived with a different bodyguard. But she had her Russian tea. Her Highness ignored me, didn't even give a nod of recognition as she feasted on her smokestack of strawberry shortcake. And then she arrived again, with the entire cafeteria watching her royal steps. She did walk like a queen, her head held high, as Milton escorted the Widow to her table. Within five minutes her Lipton's arrived in the Russian tea holder with the same familiar shortcake. It had become a ritual. That day, I wasn't really watching the Widow. I was in the midst of sketching a young married couple in slightly rumpled clothes who were having their honeymoon meal at the Belevedere. But I was interrupted. Milton loomed over me and slapped the charcoal stick out of my hand.

"Pay attention, kid. The Widow wants you at her table."

I was furious. And I had three Wolves and one Wolverine sitting beside me.

"Milton, are you blind? I'm busy."

His disposition changed. After all, we were his watchmen. I was on patrol outside the cafeteria's revolving door several times a week.

He clasped his hands together. "Then do me the kindness of visiting Madame Silverstein. She has requested your immediate company."

I scooped up the charcoal stick and walked as slowly as

I could to the Widow's table with all the swagger of the Wolves. I stopped and bowed in front of her.

"Your Highness, your wish is my command."

She looked up with a forkful of shortcake in her hand. "Child, don't get cute. I can have you killed."

"In front of all these witnesses?" I asked, playing Hamlet at the Belevedere.

"Stop it," she said. "I need your talent."

"Rosalind, I have none."

She smiled with some shortcake in her mouth. "You're a modest brat. Remember, I went to M & A. You have all the talent I'll ever need."

And she told me what it was about. The Silverstein mortuary chapel wanted an artist in

residence.

I quivered a bit under my burgundy and blue. "Rosalind, I don't know how good I am at

drawing dead people."

The Widow continued to eat and drink. "That's not the point. You'll do mementos."

She put several photographs of young men and women on the table, given to her by the widows of those "customers" Silverstein & Co. had prepared for burial. It unsettled me. The young men and women in the photographs seemed very frozen. They had all been posed by professional photographers, with fake backgrounds meant to be "picturesque"—palm trees, palace lawns, mountains, yachts. Their clothes looked ridiculous. The men had spats and starched collars that nearly covered their chins and the women had dresses with enormous shoulder pads and boots with long laces that must have been in style forty years ago. They belonged in a scrapbook, embalmed while still alive.

"Rosalind," I said, "you already have your mementos."

"No, child, I want intimacy. Not the inertia of a studio. Sketch these departed men and women in your style."

"That's the problem. I don't have much of a style."

She took a sip of Russian tea. "Yes you do, child. You just don't know it yet."

WE SETTLED ON a price for each memento, or I should say, it was Rosalind who settled—ten dollars per sketch. And I had to create my own paradise in charcoal for the sketches I produced. My favorite paradise was the Belevedere. I put all of Rosalind's young ghosts in the cafeteria. I got rid of the high collars and the laced-up boots. I drew Rosalind's subjects in a modern setting, my own time and place. I asked Milton how long the cafeteria had been there, under the El—since 1923, he said. There had been changes, "facelifts," as he called them. There had once been an enormous clock on the rear wall, and parquet on the floor rather than linoleum. The pillars had been repainted a dozen times. The Belevedere had closed for a month during each "facelift." The fluorescent lights had removed all the shadows from the walls. The size of the counter had doubled. I didn't care. I reimagined the cafeteria according to each particular ghost. It was now *my* Belevedere.

I did everything in charcoal. I captured the faces as I pleased. I looked at a photograph and let my mind drift. I couldn't really tell if my subjects were recognizable or not. Sometimes I put a band with saxophones near the revolving door. I had my ghosts dance with other ghosts. Rosalind loved whatever I did. "More," she said with a shiver in her voice.

And suddenly I had become the first professional artist in the freshman class. I gave most of the money I got to Mom.

"Anita, maybe now you can work less shifts."

She cried when I gave her the first bonanza of ten-dollar bills.

"But you earned it," she said.

"Ah, Anita, it's nothing—ghosts in a cafeteria."

I had to get working papers. Now, with a job, I could get a Social Security number. I was identifiable. I had to miss some study dates with Merle. The Widow grew more and more possessive. She wanted me inside her shop—the funeral parlor—where I occupied an alcove near her office. I didn't always draw the dead. She had me sketch her friends and business partners at Silverstein's. She might have pulled me out of school if I hadn't gone to Music and Art. She respected the Castle on the Hill too much. I had much more status now that I accompanied her to the Belevedere and sat at her table. Like her late husband, she owed a lot of money. But the Delancey Street loan sharks didn't bother Rosalind. Soon I realized why. She was related to "Delancey Street," as the niece of a loan shark. She never talked about her late husband and why he had disappeared. But it did slip out. She had a shouting match with him at the Belevedere and the next day he was gone. I admired Rosalind. She maneuvered in a world of men.

I did my homework in the alcove. I went to class. I kept all my study dates with Merle. I had dinner with the Messengers as often as I could. I never missed a midnight patrol. I observed the terrain. The Silver Wolves were really foot soldiers. Rosalind ruled this hemisphere of the South

Bronx. Even Captain Shelly was beholden to her. He paid homage to the Widow. Visited her table at the Belevedere. The captain kissed her hand. They didn't have to exchange words. They wouldn't have spilled any secrets in front of me.

I was blunt with her. And she liked that. "Rosalind, how did you get so big?"

"Clever boy," she said. "I don't meddle, I don't mix in. I settle disputes between warring parties who don't really want to go to war. I have my rewards. There's only one memorial chapel in the neighborhood—for good reason. No realtor in his right mind would offer a lease to another mortician."

I didn't ask any other questions. Michael had once been a broker like Rosalind, who brought hostile gangs to the table. But he told me never to learn what I didn't need to learn, or I might get my face busted. So I stayed out of the Widow's business affairs. I was in my alcove less and less. I drew ghosts for a living, but I went to Music and Art.

TEN

The Storyteller

Maybe it was the Messengers. I'm not sure. But I began to enjoy school for the first time in my life. I'd always been a lousy student, cutting class after class. But things would become much more complicated and confusing after I came to the Castle on the Hill. I had a sweetheart, even though I still never saw her outside our study dates and dinners at the Messengers, and our classes together at Music and Art.

I wasn't indifferent to Merle—I was frightened of her brilliance. And I couldn't keep up with her. I tried. She'd read every book in her father's library, and had accumulated a library of her own, with shelf after shelf. I didn't even have a bookcase at home. I had to read on the sly, when I was at the Belevedere, or in my alcove at the funeral parlor, and I would reflect while I was patrolling the darkened streets at the edge of Crotona Park.

But my alliances were shifting. I cared about the Wolves. And I liked my cache of ten-dollar bills and the attention I got whenever I arrived at the Belevedere with Rosalind.

I drew the ghosts for her in a cafeteria setting, and added mirrors and chandeliers as my imagination beckoned. Yet nothing excited me more than Mr. Merriman's English class. He was a maverick in polished shoes. He'd published his first novel a month before the Japanese attacked Pearl Harbor. It sold 557 copies, he said. None of his friends and fellow writers could find a copy of *Jonathan's Journey* in a bookshop.

Mr. Merriman wouldn't tell us what his lost novel was about. We all looked for it at our local libraries, but it wasn't even listed. *Jonathan's Journey* fell out of time. Dr. Merriman went back to school. He became a sub, who filled in once or twice a week for regular teachers who got sick. He lived on bread and cheese, hoping to finish a second novel. But once he arrived at the Castle on the Hill, he fell in love with the students and stayed, clawing his way to a permanent position.

"What happened to your second novel?" I asked.

"I'm still writing it," he said. "It's been fifteen years."

"Will you ever finish the novel?" asked Myrna Lippman, the poet laureate of the class.

"Doubt it," he said. Mr. Merriman shut his eyes tight for a second. "But I still have the same sensation I had when I wrote the first sentence of my first novel."

"And what sensation is that?" asked the poet laureate, as if she were tracking a lion on the loose.

"A pleasure to die for—like a samurai warrior."

He was always talking about samurai warriors, and the absolute devotion they had to their code of honor.

For a minute I thought Merriman was reckless writing sentence after sentence that flew into the same empty space as *Jonathan's Journey*. But I was wrong. He wasn't reckless at all. He loved to teach and encouraged us all to write. He was a warrior, devoted to his teaching, devoted to us. He had time for little else. We never asked him if he was married, or if he had children of his own. How could he? He was always there for us.

"Jonah," he said, "you must write every day." I did. Not with a typewriter, like the other kids in the class. I could have sat down at Merle's electric typewriter, but I didn't have the strokes—it seemed like wizardry, as her fingers flew across the keyboard. I preferred to write by hand.

I wrote about my visit to Creedmoor. Mr. Merriman scribbled "A+" at the top and had me read my composition aloud. None of the other students had ever been near a mental hospital. I exaggerated a little. But I hooked on to every detail I could recall. Patients wandering around in bathrobes, babbling to themselves; others carrying suitcases that contained their burial clothes; Michael arriving from Castle Billy in chains. I left out certain characters and situations. I didn't want the class to realize the hold that a particular police captain had on Michael and me.

"Jonah," asked Charlie Miller, who never opened his mouth in class. "Who gave your brother permission to leave his island jail? I thought he was sitting under a life sentence."

I'd slandered Charlie. He was pretty shrewd for such a silent boy. I had to fib while I was in front of the class. I said that the commandant at Castle Billy had been in touch with the chief attendant of Pop's ward, and that the two of them had worked out a deal. The hospital would send a doctor over to Castle Billy, and in return, the commandant would allow my bother to enter Creedmoor in chains, with a pair of military cops at his side. The kids wanted to know if I had been there.

"Yeah," I said, with the hurt of that memory still in my mind. "Pop was so happy to see Michael that he peed in his pants. You know, some of the patients in Pop's ward have to wear diapers, because they dribble a lot."

Another English teacher would have stopped me right there, but Mr. Merriman said that we should never skip the details, that the "pith" of a story was stuck in the details.

It was Merle who understood the danger point for me. "Jonah, how did your father react to Michael's visit?"

"Pop was overjoyed. He didn't look at me once. I didn't exist the moment he saw Michael."

"Excellent," Mr. Merriman said. "Jonah, you have the pith of your narrative right there. Your father has put you in an impossible situation."

It was worse than that. It made me jealous of Michael, and my big brother was the only reason I had been able to thrive. He'd failed to get into Music and Art, and it seemed as if I'd climbed right over his back and left him behind. He was at Castle Billy, and I was at another castle, writing about my adventures with him.

I did a second composition about Michael for Mr. Merriman and my English class. I told how my brother had discovered the silver wolf. I found the "pith" of the story, thanks to Mr. Merriman. I described how Michael had scrubbed and scrubbed the wounded wolf until that silver coat appeared.

Reading my compositions aloud soon became a class custom.

"I believe my brother knew all along what he would find

under all that blood and grime. He'd imagined the silver streaks before they ever appeared."

"Jonah," Charlie Miller said, "couldn't your brother have kept that silver wolf as a pet?"

"Silly boy," said Myrna Lipmann, "you can't keep a wolf as a pet in New York City. The law wouldn't allow it."

Charlie turned glum. "Why not?"

The poet laureate tilted her head. "Because wolves are wild. That wolf could have licked Jonah's hand one day and bit it off the next."

Charlie had a brainstorm. "You mean wolves aren't reliable."

"Yes," our poet laureate said with a smirk.

She wrote about her time at summer camp in a place called the Poconos. She read aloud to the class, like I had done. But Myrna was much more dramatic. She had all the gifts of a poet laureate. She described her first kiss. She was fourteen, and the boy, Carlton Westbrook the Fourth, was a junior life guard. His father owned the camp. Carlton was tall and had broad shoulders, Myrna said. But he wasn't born in the Bronx. So Carlton seemed like an alien to me.

"I closed my eyes," Myrna recited like an actress. "His lips were moist."

"Was it a soul kiss?" Charlie Miller asked.

"Never!" Myrna said. "He didn't have that privilege."

It hardly mattered what Myrna recited or wrote. Summer camp was nothing compared to Creedmoor and Castle Billy. The class loved my tales about the Silver Wolves and our territorial disputes. And I wrote about the Belevedere. I called it "The Queen's Cafeteria." I gave Rosalind a fictitious name. But I described the awesome power she had at the Belevedere, and also the drawings I did.

Even Myrna was impressed. "Jonah, you brought people back from the dead."

"Not really," I told the class. "It was like a trick. And the Cafeteria Queen profited from my drawings."

"Then why did you do it?" Mr. Merriman asked.

"For the money." And then I started to reflect. It was more than having cash in my pocket for me and Mom. My art, as meager as it was, had become like a magic mirror. Charcoal sticks could bring no one back from the dead. But I did have fun recreating the cafeteria according to my own plan and filling it with people from Rosalind's photographs.

"Sir," I said to Mr. Merriman. "The money was important. That's how the Cafeteria

Queen enticed me. But I had a chance to build my own Belevedere. No one could have more pleasure than that."

I had become the class storyteller. I received the grade of "100" on my report card for Mr. Merriman's class. My other grades also improved. Merle coached me a lot. We spoke French at the dinner table. I stumbled along, but I did improve.

My academic average wasn't as high as Merle's. But it had gone from 89 to 92.5. That was as close to the stratosphere as I could get. I was now one of Music and Art's academic wizards, a wise man of the freshman class. Sophomores and seniors were nicer to me. Mr. Merriman had recommended that I take his next English class, where trainees like myself and members of the staff, mostly juniors, worked as a team on *Overtone*, M & A's official newspaper. I would be a cub reporter, as Mr. Merriman called it. I had a hundred other obligations, but I agreed to join *Overtone* in the fall. Merle would also be a cub reporter. I didn't want to miss out, even if I had Captain Shelly on my back and a brother who might have to sit in chains for the rest of his life.

I dreamt of Michael. I dreamt of wolves.

SUMMER VACATION HIT me like a blizzard. I missed my Castle on the Hill. I missed Merriman. I missed Merle. She went away to summer camp, not in the Poconos, but on another mountain range in Pennsylvania. She wrote me letters. Sometimes I got two a day.

My Darling Muscular Boy,

I do not know how I will survive without you.
I'm studying archery, but it's hard to wield a bow.
I have made friends, but none as handsome as you.
If you don't write, I will never forgive you.
Tell me tales the way you told them in Merriman's class.
I want to know about the pirates who are your brothers in arms.
I want to know about your real brother and your visits to Castle Billy.
I want to know about your father in the psych ward and your mother at her chocolate factory.

Love from your favorite fiancée

Of course, I wrote back, but not with Merle's regularity. Rosalind kept me busy at the Belevedere. Her clients savored my drawings and wanted more and more pictures of the loved ones they had lost. I had less time to write. But I did have dinner with the Messengers. They told me that

Merle was at a camp for girls with disabilities. So I had to be the handsomest boy on Merle's mountain—because there weren't any boys at all.

Michael was in solitary again. Pop went into a deeper ward. The doctors there were feeding him a new drug—Thorazine. It was supposed to calm his "irrational fits," as one of the keepers on his ward said. Everyone at Creedmoor spoke of Thorazine. They called it a miracle drug. But I didn't see many miracles. I saw men and women who shuffled about in their bathrobes with a zombie's broken walk.

Pop looked the same as always. He didn't shuffle. He had that old familiar frown.

"Where's Michael?"

"Pop," I said, "he's in the brig at Castle Billy."

My father stared at me with his bloodshot eyes. "I have a dope for a son. There are no brigs on dry land. You need a ship. I learned that at the Brooklyn Navy Yard."

"Are they feeding you Thorazine?"

He laughed. I saw his yellow teeth. "That stuff's like candy. It will never harm me."

Pop gathered up the skirts of his robe and returned to his ward.

The next time I saw him he could barely utter a word. He whimpered a lot. There was a mad glaze in his eyes. But he was as docile as a ragdoll. Pop's keeper had to wipe the spittle from his chin. Pop didn't ask about Michael or about Mom. The Thorazine had whacked the life out of him. Pop could have been back in his armchair on Minford Place. But he'd never whimpered in that chair. He was sobbing now.

I wish I could have brought Michael to him on a magic carpet. That carpet belonged to Captain Shelly and it wasn't for sale. And I'm not sure the captain could have hustled the commandant at Castle Billy a second time.

Pop's robe was in tatters. His hair hadn't been combed in a month. It stood up like tilted spikes. His keeper was snoring beside him. So I took out my pocket comb, reached over the table, and flattened the spikes. Pop sat like a child as I combed his hair. And I wept like a child, because Pop would never go to the Navy Yard again, would never repair a Pontiac or a Chevrolet again, the master mechanic who had lost his gift, or left it lying around somewhere in a back ward.

That's how my summer went.

ELEVEN

Overtone

Didn't see my favorite fiancée again until the first day of class. Merle had gone to Europe with her mom and pop straight from summer camp. They flew on a plane called the Pan American Clipper, with seats that could tilt back and turn into beds. Merle's father and mother had invited me on the trip.

"We'd love to have you come along," David said.

I was shaking, and even now I'm not sure why. "I can't, David. It's so expensive, the Clipper and all."

He laughed. "It's just a plane, Jonah, just a plane. And Flora's coming, so why not you?"

I hadn't forgotten Flora, the family's major domo who'd gone to college with Mrs. Messenger. But I hesitated for a moment.

"I'd feel a bit like a beggar, sir."

"Nonsense," he said. "There are no beggars here. It would be a surprise—and such a delight for Merle."

David talked of renting a country house in Spain, in a region called Asturias. The house had its own lake, a chicken coop, and a barn with horses. It was near Gijón, "a medieval town," as David put it.

I was confused. "A medieval town? David, what does that mean?"

"It means the twentieth century hasn't come to Gijón. It thrives in its own isolation. Families take long walks after dinner. Husbands and wives hold hands. There are no American tourists—none."

"Then how did you find Gijón?"

"It was ten years ago. The Germans had surrendered. I was part of Ike's victory team in Paris. Suddenly I was on leave and had nowhere to go. I wandered around in a jeep. I saw desolation everywhere until I crossed into Spain. Spain had danced around with Hitler but remained neutral. I didn't know how I would feel in a country that had wiggled out of the war. And then I landed in Gijón. I saw the women in their mantillas."

"David, what's a mantilla?"

He smiled at the memory he was dragging out of his soldier years. "It's a long black scarf—a veil. Married women wear them so that other men may not look into their eyes. It would have caused a scandal in Gijón, even a sword fight."

I didn't believe him. "Men carry swords in Gijón?"

"I can't remember. But it seemed so. Citizens who had never left Asturias in their lives were curious about a *Yanqui* in a jeep. They invited me into their homes. I had paella with them and a custard called flan."

I didn't know what paella was and I'd never had flan. "Did the women still wear mantillas at home?"

"Of course. I was the caballero who'd come from another continent. But I never forgot Gijón and

Asturias—flowerbeds along the boulevards; the incredible slowness of time. No one ever hurries in Gijón. Jonah, can't I invite you to join us?"

I could stare into a wolf's eyes, but I was frightened of a free ride on the Clipper. And

how could I leave Mom all alone on Minford Place?

The words just jumped out. "I can't come, David. I can't."

I wasn't wearing a mantilla, and David must have seen the dread in my eyes. He didn't speak of Gijón again . . .

Merle kissed me when she came into class. She must have enjoyed the sun in Asturias. She had a terrific tan. The other students pretended not to notice the kiss, particularly the staff of *Overtone*. The rest of us were cubs.

Phyllis Pearl, the editor-in-chief, had an iron grip over the class, including Mr. Merriman. She'd already had opinion pieces accepted in several newspapers. Her photograph appeared in a magazine called *Mademoiselle*. She'd been written about in *Time* magazine, and the rumor was that recruiters from Radcliffe, Harvard's sister college, had practically guaranteed her admission into a future freshman class.

Phyllis didn't have fancy credentials. Both her parents were high school teachers. Phyllis lived with them in Parkchester, a housing development in the middle of the Bronx for families that weren't too rich or too poor. Her apartment house was at the edge of the complex, near Castle Hill Avenue. I'd been to Parkchester several times with the Silver Wolves, as we raced across the Bronx in our colors. Parkchester reminded me of an enchanted version of Creedmoor, a city within a city. Parkchester didn't have people walking around in bathrobes. It was filled with gardens and ponds and green gates. I'd always dreamt that we would move into that complex, away from the constant rattle of the El and piles of garbage in the streets. But I doubt that a silver wolf ever roamed the gardens, or that Parkchester had a gang of its own.

I never saw a single Black family in that complex. That's what Phyllis had written about in her opinion piece, how Black families had been discriminated against by the complex, and how Parkchester had an "exclusion clause." It wouldn't rent to Black families. And Phyllis had exposed that.

Phyllis was a fighter. She was curt with the class. And Merriman allowed her to rule as editor-in-chief.

"Cubbies," she said to her new crop of reporters, "we aren't going to lick the heels of the Parents' Association. We aren't assembled here to satisfy or entertain. We are going to inform. *Overtone* isn't a rotogravure. It will deliver news. And I don't care if we get into trouble. Mr. Merriman will bail us out."

"I'll try," Merriman told the class.

Phyllis whipped her head back. "Oh, you'll have to do much more than that, or we'll never survive as a newspaper. And we'll end up as a commonplace rotogravure, a silly sheet."

A rotogravure, I soon learned, was the illustrated section of the Sunday paper with all the fancy ads that were poison to Phyllis.

She had very thick glasses, and she liked to wear the same sweatshirt to every class. She was barely five feet tall. *Time* had called her "a sizzler."

And she was.

Phyllis expected all the cub reporters to be "newshounds," to come up with amazing stories that she could then feature in

Overtone. But Phyllis didn't train her cubs. She would rewrite every sentence we wrote. We were still very eager to learn.

"Jonah," she said, "I hear your older brother is locked away at Castle Billy for life. Is that true?"

Who had told her about Michael? Merle would never have snitched.

"Yes, Phyllis. It's true."

"Well," she said, "what are you waiting for? Can't you sniff out a story? The older brother of a Music and Arter condemned to a military prison a short ferry ride away from Manhattan? And wasn't he the leader of a notorious gang, the White Wolves?"

"Silver Wolves," I said.

"Ah," she said, "better still. I like the ring of that. *Silver Wolves*. Jonah, aren't you listening? Take another cub and interview your brother."

We all looked at Mr. Merriman. "The Parents Association will slaughter us," he warned.

"Why?" Phyllis growled.

"They'll say it's sordid. But we'll survive, and then there's the dean's wrath to consider."

"Oh," Phyllis said, "I'll deal with Dean Moss."

Amanda Moss was Music and Art's academic dean. Everyone was afraid of her except Phyllis, who was beyond Amanda's reach ever since she'd been mentioned in *Time* as one of the top ten high school students in the whole United States. But the dean had put herself in charge of whatever went into *Overtone*, and I knew there would be a clash. And I would have to pay the price. But Phyllis Pearl was impossible to resist.

I RODE THE ferry with my fiancée. We huddled under the shivering roof of the main deck in the midst of a storm. The ferry rocked in its channel. The wind blew us off our seats. We sat on the wet floor, our shoes soaked. It took ten minutes for the ferry to dock. That was almost as long as the ride. We had to run up to Castle Billy with Merle's raincoat covering our heads.

We must have looked like scavengers to the military cops rather than a pair of cub reporters. The cops recognized me, but they had never met Merle. I introduced her as my cousin. She took out her passport. The captain of the guard inspected it with a magnifying glass. "It's not forged," he muttered. Then he stared at Merle with cruel delight. These military guardians were just like a gang. They didn't want their territory invaded.

"Hello, Cousin Merle," the captain said with a crooked smile.

It took a long time before Michael arrived in his chains. His cheeks were all sunken. His eyes sat deep in their sockets. But he took to Merle immediately.

I told Michael about our assignment to write about him and his captivity for *Overtone*.

He smiled and I could see the rawness of his gums. "Is your school on a crusade?"

"Michael, you could call it that," Merle said. "Our editor-in-chief is a real crusader."

Merle had come prepared. She'd brought a notebook and a Parker pen. She didn't dance around with Michael. She asked him why he was wasting away at Castle Billy.

Michael told her about the time he'd spent in Alaska, how a friendly drink with his commanding officer had ended in a drunken brawl.

Merle was a much better cub than me. She pinned Michael down. "Do ordinary soldiers usually go to bars with their commanding officers?"

"It's Anchorage, Merle. There isn't that much to do. Cap and I often got drunk together. But he was mean on this occasion. He ordered me to undress so that he could look at my tail."

"Tail, what tail?" Merle asked, utterly confused. "That doesn't make much sense,"

"It did to him," Michael told her. "He said that all Jews had tails and he wanted to look at mine. And when I refused, he hit me with a beer bottle and the brawl began."

Merle kept scribbling in her notebook. "But surely the judges must have taken that into consideration at your court martial."

Michael frowned. "They did. They reprimanded my captain and sent me home to Castle Billy."

WE WROTE THE article together and Merle typed it out on her IBM Electric. I can't say whose style it was, Merle's or mine. It was mimeographed at M & A, and we all scrutinized it together—cubs, *Overtone* editors, and Mr. Merriman. And then Phyllis edited the article with a red pencil and her gifted hand. She revised whatever we wrote, shifting paragraphs around, shortening snips of dialogue, until whatever voice Merle and I had was barely recognizable.

"Good job. I'm proud of you kids." She scribbled "—30—" in red at the bottom of the article and rasped, "Send it to the printer."

It was the lead article in the next issue of *Overtone*, with a headline that Phyllis herself prepared:

SILVER WOLF AT CASTLE BILLY

The issue went through multiple reprints. That's how much controversy the article aroused. Merle and I had our own byline—*Researched and written by sophomores Merle Messenger and Jonah Salt*.

Phyllis wouldn't grab any of the credit. "I prefer to remain invisible."

The Parents Association grumbled. There had never been a story about a military bandit and gang leader in *Overtone*. But once the parents realized how popular the issue was, that for the first time *Overtone* had readers beyond the realm of M & A, that other high schools clamored for the issue, the Parents Association ultimately decided against a formal complaint.

Dean Moss was also silent. I think she was stunned. But she marched into our classroom after the fourth printing. She berated Mr. Merriman in front of us. "Thomas, I will not abide poor judgment from a member of the faculty. Who approved such scandalous material?"

"I did," Phyllis said.

Dean Moss was apoplectic. Her ears turned red. Finally she was able to calm herself. "But you're a student, my dear."

"I'm editor-in-chief," Phyllis snapped at the dean. "I decide what is worthy to print. Jonah Salt is a student here. And his brother is condemned to Governors Island. That is news, Dean Amanda."

"Don't be disrespectful, dear," the dean said in a much lower voice. A student had challenged her authority, but Phyllis was as well-known as Willie Mays in certain circles of Manhattan and the Bronx, and the dean couldn't afford to alienate her. She would have lost the battle. And so she marched out of the room.

We all looked at Phyllis in amazement. She had torn my other writing to shreds, had hammered away at Merle, but the article that appeared in *Overtone* was more spectacular and convincing than anything we had ever written. Michael was the lone hero of *Silver Wolf at Castle Billy*, the outcast, the sufferer, the king of a Bronx neighborhood who had lost his kingdom, and was condemned by the government to sit in exile for the rest of his life. And I was his baby brother and his squire.

I had no more problems with my fellow Music and Arters. They saluted me in the halls. I, sophomore Jonah Salt, was related to the military bandit at Castle Billy.

TWELVE

The Missing Sapphire

I KNEW MY priorities. I had to sketch the living dead with my charcoal sticks for Rosalind to stay afloat. But the Cafeteria Queen saw how curious I suddenly was about the Ivy League now that my grades had spiraled. I didn't have a benefactor. I would have to convince one of the Ivies to award me a scholarship when the time was ripe. I couldn't apply as a member of the Silver Wolves or as an artist inside a funeral parlor. I would have been rejected outright. I could list my work on Overtone as a cub reporter. Admission officers would have liked that, but cubs didn't bring in any cash.

Rosalind was amused by my dilemma. "Child, I'll lend you whatever money you need."

"No, thanks, Madame Silverstein. I'm aware of what happens to people who can't repay their loans."

She laughed. "You're such a sweetheart." And I did my homework near her desk.

I didn't forget my midnight patrols. We were much weaker without Michael. We'd lost our feel of the neighborhood, the silver wolf's wandering yellow eye that

Michael had, that gift of detail. We were aliens in our own land.

It was *Overtone* that occupied me now. We'd become Phyllis' star reporters, Merle and I.

WE INTERVIEWED A diplomat at the United Nations, a captain of the Staten Island ferry, and Merle's dad at his advertising agency. David occupied a magnificent crow's nest on Madison Avenue, with balconies that wrapped around an entire floor. Merle was a shrewd questioner.

"You're the founder of your own company, Dad. What's your chief concern?"

"To make money," David said, "tons of it."

His daughter grew very severe. "But you have to compete with every other ad agency. What makes David Messenger unique?"

"We're not unique at all. We pretty much have the same formula—creativity and aggression."

"Oh, Dad," Merle said. "Can't you name a client and talk about a particular ad campaign?"

David seemed disappointed with himself as the sun beat down from his enormous window. "I couldn't do that, Merle. My clients would feel betrayed."

"Then what can you tell us?" Merle asked with a sullen look.

"I have a slight edge," David said, his sense of disappointment having softened a bit. "I'm one of the President's speechwriters. And clients like to be close to the circuitry of government."

He gave us a tour of his "shop," as he called the different studios and conference rooms. We met several of the artists and copywriters who worked on ad campaigns. None of David's artists used charcoal sticks. They all had a stash of crayons and colored pencils and sat in front of gigantic easels. One of the artists had graduated from Music and Art. He poked me with a pencil.

"It ain't Van Gogh, kid. But it's a living. This agency has punch and pizzazz."

"What's pizzazz?" I asked

"Pizzazz is pizazz," he said. "You can call it glamor, glamor and high style."

David took us to lunch at his favorite restaurant, Robbers Roost. It was where most of

the ad men ate. The Roost, as David called it, specialized in "Northern Italian cuisine." He had his own table at Robbers Roost. Other ad men kept coming over and shaking his hand. They all smiled and kissed Merle on the cheek, but I could sense a hunger and a rage beneath that smile. David's shop was more successful than theirs. He had a direct line to the White House, and they did not. He was known on Madison Avenue as "Eisenhower's Musketeer."

David ordered for the three of us. He spoke Italian to the waiters and the chef, who chatted with him and sang out each special like a male soprano. Merle whispered in my ear. Her father had to memorize a load of foreign languages as Eisenhower's aide. I'd picked up the fundamentals of using a knife and a fork on Central Park West. So I was fine at Robbers Roost.

We started out with roasted tomatoes on crusts of bread sprinkled with olive oil. The name of that appetizer was too hard to pronounce. Then we had tuna fish that was better than any tuna that ever came out of a can and spinach that was molded into a ball. We all had a wallop of black coffee afterwards in little porcelain cups with almond macaroons on a blue plate.

"Father," Merle asked, "isn't it expensive to have your own table at Robbers Roost?"

"Yes, it is," David said. "But it's a necessary expense. I want my competitors to eat their hearts out every time they see me at this table." Merle stitched the story together for the next issue. Phyllis wasn't satisfied. "Cubby," she said, "you're too attached. You're writing about your own dad."

There was little left of Merle in the article Phyllis rewrote. She called David's shop "part of the capitalist empire." This time Dean Moss arrived before the copy went to the printer. She wagged the page proofs of the next issue in front of the class.

"Phyllis Pearl, you may be editor-in-chief, but I can strip you of that title and shut down *Overtone*. You will not call Madison Avenue and all its advertising agencies a capitalist empire with a policy of dog-eat-dog—not while I am the dean. The Parents Association would destroy us all."

"I resign," Phyllis said.

The dean was on the verge of a panic attack. "Now, Phyllis, don't be rash. You have become the heartbeat of *Overtone*."

Phyllis fought back. "Didn't we write about Merle's father? Isn't that news?"

The dean was still distraught. "But you practically decapitated him and his agency, dear."

Phyllis peered at the dean from behind her thick lenses. "You can't decapitate an agency, Ma'am. It isn't grammatical."

"Grammatical or not," the dean said, "that mention of 'dog eat dog' has to be stricken from the article."

Phyllis erased all her red pencil marks and restored what Merle and I had written. She must have understood that her position on *Overtone* was her seat of power, and she didn't want to give it up. She loved barking orders and calling us her "cubbies."

Merle and I had our byline, and David's photo was on the front page. Phyllis had picked the title: THE LIFE OF AN ADVERTISING BARON.

David seemed satisfied with the article. The Parents Association thanked Dean Moss, the entire staff, and particularly Phyllis Pearl. But Phyllis seemed much more aloof and less interested in her "cubbies." As time went on, there were fewer and fewer red pencil marks.

SARAH SUGARMAN WAS one of the cubs. She was also a debutante. She lived on Park Avenue with all the Sugarmans, who had their own chain of hotels. They were the kings of Florida, lords of Palm Beach. Sarah was already engaged at sixteen. She wasn't much of a cub, but she did have an engagement ring. She showed it off to her girlfriends at M & A. Sarah's ring had a bunch of little diamonds embedded in a band of white gold with a blue stone in the middle—the stone, Sarah said, was a sapphire worth thousands of dollars. One morning she left the ring in her locker while she was in gym class. And when she returned from gym, her ring with the blue sapphire was gone. A thief had broken into her locker and had ripped the door right off its hinge. The thief must have used a crowbar. But how could the thief have gotten past the matron outside the girls' locker room? Dean Amanda didn't have a choice. The cops were called in. Two detectives arrived from Police Headquarters on Centre Street in grey fedoras, the same hat Pop used to wear until he was sent to Creedmoor, a hat with a silk ribbon and a slightly dented crown. None of the patients at the asylum wore hats.

As cub reporters, we were permitted to follow the detectives around. They were very thorough and very fast. They were convinced that the culprit was a member of the janitorial staff. Records were dug up from the files in the basement. One of the janitors, Stefan, who was born in Belgium, had spent some time in the Tombs, the dreaded jail in lower Manhattan that was as bad for adults as Spofford was for juveniles. Stefan was there on an assault and battery charge, and was later released. Assault and battery had little to do with a crowbar in the girls' locker room, but the two detectives still brought Stefan downtown for questioning. I watched his shoulders slump. His English wasn't perfect. Who would be there to defend him? He was put on leave until the matter was cleared. I noticed the look of glee under the detectives' fedoras. They had their man. It was shameful. Stefan couldn't have gotten into the girl's locker room without being noticed. And the matron hadn't noticed him.

That didn't matter to Phyllis. She sniffed a story, and assigned it to her star reporters. Merle and I didn't have many clues. We both realized that Stefan had been snatched from Music and Art for the sake of convenience, so that the two "fedoras" could pretend they had cracked the case. We went to Merle's dad. David said we would need an exact description of the ring. "And get a picture of the girl who lost it."

"Why?" I asked.

David rolled his eyes. "Just get it."

So we met with Sarah after class. Merle had her father's Polaroid. Sarah sulked, since her fiancé's jeweler had fashioned the sapphire for her wedding finger. "The ring's insured, Jonah. But it can't be replaced. It's one of a kind. I should never have left it in the locker. That was reckless of me." Merle took Sarah's picture with the Polaroid while we talked. And Merle had drawn an image of Sarah's sapphire from memory, since Sarah had shown it to everyone at M & A who would look at her ring.

"Don't tell Charles," she said. Charles was her fiancé, now a sophomore at the Wharton School of Business. We considered traveling to Philadelphia to meet her fiancé at Wharton. But we decided against it. We were cub reporters, not two "fedoras." But Sarah did give us the name of the jeweler in Manhattan where the ring was made. It wasn't in the Diamond District, a mad bazaar of stores and stands on 47th Street, packed with people; so many hawkers and clients—buyers sellers, and tourists—that there wasn't much space to breathe on the sidewalk. But Sarah's store was downtown, on Maiden Lane, in the old, half-forgotten Diamond District. There was no jewelry in the window of Barley & Son. There was no display window at all. We had to climb three flights to get to the ring-maker. It was a struggle for Merle, so I carried her up the second and third flight.

The ring-maker was nineteen, a prodigy, an apprentice who was also a master craftsman. He wouldn't tell us his name. "I'm not allowed," he said. "Mr. Barley's worried that someone might steal me away." But he did show us the sketches for Sarah Sugarman's engagement ring, a dozen of them. He couldn't give us the actual sketches, but Sarah captured them with her father's Polaroid.

He hadn't gone to Music and Art, this boy master. He'd studied jewelry at the High School of Industrial Art. It was a trade school that was shunned by the brightest students because it did not award an academic diploma. Michael had gone there after his grades plummeted while he was warlord of the Silver Wolves. He also studied jewelry—and watch repair—at Industrial Art. But this boy was hired by Barley & Son when he was a sophomore, and he'd been with Barley ever since.

"I remember the Sugarman girl," he said. "She knew the ring she wanted, and I built it for her. But the blue sapphire was my idea."

"How much did the ring cost?" Merle asked.

"Oh, I never price the merchandise," the boy said. "Mr. Barley uses his adding machine—his material and my labor. Three thousand would be my guess. I'm sorry. I couldn't get you the actual receipt. That's strictly confidential."

Merle persisted. "Did Sarah Sugarman like her engagement ring?"

"She worshipped it," the boy said. "She wouldn't let it off her finger."

WE KEPT AWAY from the "fedoras" and went straight to Captain Shelly. We showed him Merle's Polaroids, revealing the ring-maker's sketches of Sarah's engagement ring. "Where's the knish?" he asked.

Merle wasn't familiar with the captain's slang. A knish was actually a piece of fried dough stuffed with baked potato, wolfed down at delicatessens in the Bronx and on Manhattan's Lower East Side. But in Shelly's slang it meant a girl, in particular a girl with a sense of mystery, a sense of the unknown.

Merle gave him the picture of Sarah that she took with her father's Polaroid. The captain squinted. "Quite a knish. And I suppose the ring in question is an engagement ring, worth its weight in gold?"

"And sapphires," I said. "One blue sapphire."

Shelly looked at both of us. "And the ring was misplaced?"

"Left in her locker while she went to gym," I said.

Shelly rubbed his hands together. "Beautiful. And while the knish was in her gym class, her locker was broken into, and the ring disappeared. Give me a week."

It took the captain two days. He had Sarah's sapphire wrapped in a piece of fine tissue paper. He didn't gloat.

"Cap," I said, "where did you find Sarah Sugarman's ring?"

"At a pawnshop on Eighth Avenue. The knish will have to fork over half a grand to the pawnbroker."

I was bewildered. "He gave you back the ring?"

"I grabbed it," Captain Shelly said. "It's evidence, ain't it? The ring was reported stolen.

But the pawnbroker will have to be repaid, or the knish will end up in court."

And so we returned the ring to Sarah Sugarman in the same fancy tissue paper. She seemed startled. But I noticed a slight quiver in her cheek. I was junior detective Jonah Salt.

I could see how fine an actress Sarah was. "My God," she said, "how on earth did you come up with my engagement ring? You must both be miracle workers. I'll have to tell Charles."

Merle shoved politeness aside. "Sarah, it had nothing to do with miracles. You bartered your precious ring with a pawnbroker."

"I did not," Sarah insisted. Then she looked into Merle's eyes and let her big act slide.

"I was desperate."

"You're a Sugarman," Merle said. "Your allowance is probably as big as our school's budget."

"I'm pregnant," Sarah whispered. And the air seemed to shift. I became unsettled. But Merle was a much better soldier than I. Unchanged in her resolve, she said, "How can we help?" I should've known she wouldn't leave Sarah stranded.

Sarah began to mumble. "I can't tell Mother. She'd have a nervous breakdown. And Dad would disown me or worse."

"What about Charles?" Merle asked. "Isn't he a financial wizard at Wharton?"

"Some wizard," Sarah said. "He lost whatever loot I had in the bank gambling on the stock market. So I didn't have much of a choice. I had to hock the ring. Or I couldn't pay the Barber. He performs abortions."

THE BARBER RAN a shady abortion clinic on South Street, close to the ferry slip. He must have been a quack who had lost his medical license. I asked Rosalind about him. But she had never heard about the Barber of South Street. So we were all in the dark.

Charles, the financial wizard, wasn't willing to accompany Sarah. He couldn't risk his standing at Wharton. The engagement was called off. Sarah was one of the girls who had mocked Merle and her disability, but Merle wouldn't punish her for that. She was as resourceful as her dad. She arranged it so that Sarah would be the Messengers' guest after the ordeal was over.

I wondered whether I should bring some of the Silver Wolves to South Street with us. But Merle was against it. She said it would attract too much attention. So the three of us went alone. I still wore my colors. We rode in a cab to a deserted barbershop right near the ferry slip to Governors Island. I could see the empty barber chairs through the shop window and the bottles of hair tonic lined up on a narrow shelf. We didn't have to knock. A woman came to the door wearing a smock stained with blood. She didn't hide her contempt. Sarah had to pay her in advance. The woman counted the bills in front of us. She let Sarah and Merle into the shop, but I had to wait outside. She locked the door.

Wicked thoughts whipped through my head. I wanted to raid the barbershop and get Sarah and Merle out of there. I felt helpless outside, anxious. What if the Barber was a fraud and the woman with the blood stains was his accomplice in crime? I knew this made no sense. The woman had already collected her swag from Sarah. Still, I could do nothing but wait.

It grew dark on the docks. The last ferry to Governors Island had gone and returned. The ferry sat there, rocking in the water. I thought of Michael spilling his blood and guts at Castle Billy. I thought of Mom dipping cherries in a pool of chocolate from sunrise to sunset. I thought of Pop in a back ward of the asylum, his mind in a Thorazine fog. And while I was deep in my own bewilderment, Merle came out of the barbershop with Sarah behind her. I couldn't even tell how long they'd been inside. I hadn't glanced at my Timex. Sarah's cheeks were the color of chalk, or else she could have been wearing a mask that was painted white. I didn't dally. I hailed a cab . . .

Sarah was back at school with her sapphire ring after two days. The pale white mask was gone. Merle and I had helped her forge a letter of absence. But Sarah didn't feel beholden to us or to Stefan the janitor, who never got his job back at M & A. He was banished to a school in the outer boroughs.

Our editor-in-chief was itching to reveal the mystery behind Sarah's stolen sapphire. So she interviewed Sarah herself. And Sarah lied and lied about the ring. Phyllis was clever enough to see through Sarah's lies, and quickly conclude she couldn't print the story. This was different from the others. It would have caused so much of a stink that her own name could have been sullied. And besides, Sarah's father was a major supporter of the Parents Association. The dean would have demoted Phyllis and destroyed an entire issue of *Overtone*. I thought about Stefan and how he had been swindled out of a job at M & A. It cut into my image of a cub reporter. It seemed less glorious now. But I was stubborn, as stubborn and wild as a silver wolf.

II
LOST AND FOUND

THIRTEEN

Broken Bones

Maybe it was inevitable. Maybe not. Merle had permission to arrive several minutes late for every class, to walk in the halls when it wasn't crowded with students wandering from room to room. But she didn't want to be hampered by the late bell. We had pretty much the same schedule, so I escorted her from one class to the next. But one afternoon, we stayed a few minutes late after our journalism class to discuss with Phyllis and Mr. Merriman an article we meant to write about M & A's free lunch program. The topic was taboo, since the free lunchers weren't happy about identifying themselves, and the dean didn't want them identified in *Overtone*, but our editor-in-chief was adamant. Poverty was always on her mind. And she wanted it mentioned openly. I suspect that Mr. Merriman agreed with her, but he preferred to remain in the background.

"Poverty abounds," Phyllis declared. I'm not sure what she meant, but I loved the sound of what she said. So, we were late for our next class. We could have grabbed the faculty elevator—Merle had permission to do so—but the elevator car seemed stuck on a lower floor, and we had to climb down a flight of stairs. But we weren't lucky. Students were rushing to their next class, trying to avoid the late bell. One of them, an upperclassman, was more than careless. He banged into me on his way up to the next landing. It seemed like a deliberate shove. I tripped, and Merle fell down the flight of stairs, her arms flailing, as the cane leapt into the air. I was hypnotized for a moment, as I followed the flying cane, horrified that I had failed Merle and wasn't able to help. I was so befuddled that the scene began to take on a kind of hazy atmosphere. Time slowed. Even now, the memory that the sound of our bodies made hitting the floor, the gasps that careened throughout the hallway—they take on a dreamlike quality, like they were happening elsewhere, to other people, in a different realm. I don't remember how long I remained on the ground but suddenly I was upright, watching Merle get wheeled out of the school. A sharp pain ripped through my body.

I couldn't ride in the ambulance with her. I wasn't a relative. So I took the train to the French Hospital on the West Side of Manhattan. The matrons wouldn't let me in to see Merle until David and Alice appeared. I could read the terror in their eyes.

"What hap—pened, Jonah?" David asked in a broken voice.

"Merle fell down a flight of stairs."

His mouth twitched with anger. "Why the hell was she using stairs in the first place?"

"We were late for class, David. The elevator was stuck, and—"

"You could have waited with her. You could have waited." His anger was much more deliberate.

Alice touched his sleeve. "We shouldn't dawdle, David. We have to go in to see our daughter. It's not Jonah's fault. He was looking after her, dear. He was trying to protect her."

"He should have tried harder," David muttered. And then his anger went deep inside himself and he put his arm around my shoulder. "I'm sorry, Jonah. I didn't mean. . . . I'm very upset. Music and Art should have made sure this didn't happen."

A nurse led David and Alice across a series of hallways and into the polio ward, where Merle lay in a hospital bed in a room full of iron lungs. I'd never seen an iron lung before. It looked like an enormous cannon shell decorated with little circular windows. Polio patients were entombed inside, with their faces sticking out of the shell that pushed their lungs and breathed for them. I thought they would all look like ghosts with a ghost's pale white complexion. But these patients all had red cheeks. Merle had once lived in an iron lung. But she didn't need one now. Her broken leg was in a hammock suspended above the bed. She was sedated but wasn't asleep.

"It's my fault, Dad," she said in a low voice. "I was brazen. I didn't want to be late for class."

She clutched my hand. Then her fingers fell away and she dozed off with her chin against her shoulder. The surgeon arrived. He was wearing a surgical cap and a crumpled gown with a trace of blood. He showed several x-rays to David and Alice. I was excluded from this forum. But I caught a lot of what he told them. Her already damaged leg was now fractured in several places. It would take more than one operation to set the bones in place and to have them knit together.

"Will she walk again?" David asked. "I don't want my daughter in a wheelchair for the rest of her life."

The surgeon wasn't playing poker with David. "I can guarantee you, Mr. Messenger. Her leg will be stronger than it was before the break. We've made advances since she first contracted polio. I would have advised this operation even if she hadn't fallen. Now the bones will knit in a better way."

DAVID DIDN'T ABANDON me. He invited me to dinner. Alice was much too morose to cook. It was Flora who prepared the meal. David didn't want me to visit Merle right after the operation. He preferred that I wait until she healed a bit.

"It will excite her, Jonah. And I want her to rest. I'm to blame. I sent her to summer camp while polio was rampant. It was a very elite camp. Polio-proof, the headmaster said. They hadn't reported a single case . . . until Merle. I wanted to burn that camp to the ground."

"Oh, David, "Alice said. "Would that have rescued Merle?"

David drove me home after dinner in his Cadillac convertible. We stopped on Charlotte Street, where he was born. He liked to stare at the rooftops of the tenements, at the crookedness of their line. "Jonah, should I tell you how poor we were? I had to steal from the grocery store right in front of the grocer's eyes. My father had the white plague—tuberculosis. He would spit his lungs out in a basin under the bed. I promised myself I wouldn't die on Charlotte Street, like him. It's funny, but I miss him the most, miss him every single day. I barely remember my half-brothers and sisters, my uncles or my aunts. My mother died when I was born. My father married again. But it was more like a business affair. I didn't feel any love when my new mother looked at me. She writes letters now, begging for money. I never answer."

I stared at the plush seats of the convertible. "Isn't that cruel?"

"Yes," he said. "And it was meant to be. That was Charlotte Street."

"David, what did your father do?"

"He was a painter who worked at the post office."

I'd never heard of such a thing. "A house painter?

"No," David said. "An artist—like you."

"Did he ever show his art in a gallery?"

"No," David said. "He never tried. But I have all his paintings. I keep them in a folio

bound in Moroccan leather. They sit in my clothes closet."

I grew excited. "They could be a national treasure, worth millions."

"No," David said. "They aren't very good. I had them appraised. One collector called them a mishmash of colors."

David's story disturbed me. He should have had his father's art appraised by other collectors. I couldn't interfere. What if his father was the undiscovered Rembrandt of the Bronx?

David let me off at Minford Place . . .

I wasn't much of a cub reporter without Merle. We were a team. We worked in tandem.

I couldn't thrive without her fingers on the keyboard of her electric typewriter. Phyllis gave out assignments to other cubs. I was promoted to assistant editor, but it wasn't a promotion at all. I sat around with her and Merriman, editing pieces with a red pencil.

Finally I was allowed to visit Merle. She'd endured three operations. Bones were broken and reset again. She had a cast on her leg made of plaster as hard as a rock. She didn't have to sit in a wheelchair. She could hop around on crutches. We went out onto the terrace. We could see above the roofs and rear gardens and across the grey of the Hudson River to the lights of Jersey City that looked like a long, irregular string, or a twisting snake that disappeared and appeared again and again.

We did our homework together, just as we had done on Central Park West. I would give Merle the notes I took for every class. All her teachers loved her, and they allowed me to administer Merle's exams. Her midterm grades were higher than mine. Mr. Merriman came to visit Merle at the French hospital's rehabilitation center. He seemed much less vital outside the classroom, almost withdrawn.

Merle asked him about his second novel.

"Oh, it's cooking," he said. But it wasn't cooking at all. I could tell. The classroom made him bold. He wasn't bored of teaching like some of the other teachers we had. He came alive in front of a class, moved about with a certain force. He was our very own Hamlet, plucked right out of Shakespeare.

He didn't bring Merle flowers. Flowers wouldn't have defined Mr. Merriman. He'd brought her a copy of *Jonathan's Journey*, his one and only novel. The book jacket was slightly frayed. Merle and I signaled each other with our eyes. We both knew how important a gift it was. He'd never shared his work, not once.

He borrowed Merle's Parker pen and wrote an inscription on a blank page of the book:

> *To Merle Messenger (and to Jonah,
> her comrade in arms),*
>
> *You have both given me more pleasure than I deserve.*
>
> *Humbly,
> Tom Merriman*

He didn't say much after that inscription. And he wouldn't open up to us and reveal the mystery of his private life. Maybe he couldn't. He sat quietly with us, his long fingers on his lap, and then he leapt up and kissed Merle on the little bump between her eyes.

"Come back to us as soon you can. We just can't thrive without you, Merle. We miss your cleverness and your company too much."

And then he was gone.

We didn't have a fight over who would read Merriman's book first. Merle was the patient, not I. Merle was bedridden, though that wasn't exactly true. She could navigate across the rehabilitation center with her crutches like a stranded sea captain. She let me have *Jonathan's Journey* after two days without uttering a single comment about the book.

"Read it. Then we'll talk."

And so I did.

It was the first adult novel I tried to read on my own from

beginning to end. I'd skipped passages in *A Tale of Two Cities*. Sidney Carton was the one who had interested me, the guy who could never stand on solid ground until he was standing on the guillotine.

I understood Mr. Merriman a little better after starting *Jonathan's Journey*. I can't say if the boy in the novel was a mirror of Merriman himself. Jonathan, the hero of the novel, was born in South Dakota on what was called a hardscrabble farm, a place without rich soil. Jonathan was the oldest son. His mother and father scratched and scraped from morning to midnight. Jonathan looked after his younger brothers and brought them to school, a barn that sat with a slanted roof in the middle of nowhere. It nearly flew across the plains after a hurricane. It shivered during a thunder storm. The roof leaked, and every student, from the first grade through senior class, had to carry out buckets of water. The blackboard was always wet and hardly held the teacher's chalk marks. Jonathan's school had one teacher, Miss Brown. She wasn't from South Dakota. She's never described in the novel. But she'd come from far away to teach at a one-room schoolhouse in the flatlands. It must have been like missionary work. All twenty-nine of the students sat together in the same room. And she wandered from student to student, giving out different assignments, handing out whatever books she had. She sensed how tenacious Jonathan was to learn. There were times when the boy skipped school for weeks, helping his mother and father plant crops on that bitter ground. It didn't really matter. Jonathan studied on his own. Miss Brown had him in her classroom for six years. She gave him a booklet to read. It was about a special program at the University of Chicago, where gifted students from all over the country would go to high school on the university campus, and after they graduated would "matriculate" at the university itself. I liked that word—matriculate.

Jonathan went home to the farm one afternoon with Miss Brown. She explained the program to his mother and father. Jonathan would have the very best education in America, his high school classes taught by professors from the university. His father signed the consent form. Miss Brown mailed it in with her own recommendation. Jonathan was accepted in the program. He spent his last summer on the farm, plowing that impossible earth, tying the laces of his younger brothers, combing their hair, helping his mother in the kitchen . . .

I returned the book to Merle at the rehabilitation center.

"How far did you get?" she asked.

"Page seventy-three," I said.

"Same here."

Both of us had a premonition, the same sad belief that Jonathan would never return to that farmhouse in the flatlands, that he would never see his little brothers again, never see his mother and father, never see Miss Brown. His world would become Chicago—and Manhattan, maybe.

"Why couldn't you continue?" Merle asked.

"It was too painful," I said. Perhaps we were snobs, but we could both predict how Jonathan's "journey"—his hunger for education—haunted Mr. Merriman and continued to haunt him. He would never finish his second novel. There was no novel to finish. We didn't know if Mr. Merriman had come from South Dakota, or if he ever had little brothers with wet hair to comb, but the classroom he taught in at M & A (it was always the same room) must have been a replica of the schoolhouse in *Jonathan's Journey*, at least in Merriman's mind.

FOURTEEN

Merriman & Merle

We were all startled when Merle stopped using the crutches. Both of her legs had been massaged by the hospital's best "masseurs" as they were called. Her muscle tone was more than adequate, Merle's doctor had assured the Messengers. I happened to be there. The doctor himself locked the leg brace. But the first time she tried to walk on her own, she crumpled to the ground.

"It's excitement," the doctor said, slightly embarrassed. "She's done beautifully for us, without the cane or the crutches."

She tried again, and again she flopped.

"Mr. Messenger," the doctor said, "her muscles couldn't have withered overnight."

"Charlatans," David muttered. He had Merle discharged and brought home in his Cadillac. He massaged her leg, as he had done for months, after she first contracted polio. It was David who revived Merle's muscle tone. He had specialists called in. They examined Merle. "Mr. Messenger," the latest one insisted, "the bones have healed and the muscles are tight."

But she couldn't walk across a room with David standing right behind her. She used a cane as a third leg. The cane propelled her, and she leapt rather than walked. She did not have a "gait of her own," as one of the charlatans called it.

David put his partner in charge of the ad agency, canceled his noon reservations at Robbers Roost, and worked with his daughter to get back her gait. He would gather her in his arms, dance with Merle, humming a melody out of his own childhood. She could hear her father sob. That's what Merle told me.

"I failed you," he muttered to himself.

"You did not, Dad. I could have caught polio anywhere. It was destined that way."

He was willing to hire tutors for her, but Merle wouldn't hear of it.

"Dad, I'm a Music and Arter, through and through."

And so she finally returned to the Castle after four months. Phyllis sensed that she now had a rival at *Overtone*. She tried to push Merle around. But Merle insisted.

"I want your best lead. Jonah and I still share a byline."

"Sorry, Merle," Phyllis said. "Jonah is my editorial assistant now. He rides on a red pencil."

"Give him back to me," Merle said. "And you can ride that red pencil on your own."

Mr. Merriman couldn't interfere. Phyllis was still editor-in-chief. But she surrendered to Merle. She wasn't a dope. She knew that we delivered the best stories, even if the appearance of our byline in *Overtone* often gave Dean Amanda Moss and the Parents Association a fit.

Merle wanted to interview Mr. Merriman.

I was reluctant. "You know how secretive he is about his life."

"Well, I like secrets."

Merle had a star reporter's instinct. "He's given us *Jonathan's Journey* to read. That has to mean something."

"But we never finished the book," I said.

"Jonah, be brazen for once."

And so we went to Mr. Merriman. I was stunned when he agreed to the interview.

Merle pressed him, pressed him hard. "Jonathan's journey wasn't his alone, was it, sir? You went to high school at the University of Chicago, didn't you?"

"Yes, I did."

"And you never returned to South Dakota."

"Nebraska," Merriman said. "It's the novelist's privilege to lie a little."

Merle was relentless. I didn't have her gifts. All I had to keep up with Merle was the memory of a silver wolf.

"But you are Jonathan," Merle said, "or Jonathan's double. And you never went back to Nebraska and that schoolhouse in a barn."

"I did, Merle, I did. And the school wasn't in a barn. It was in an abandoned farmhouse, and it had more than one room."

"But one teacher, Miss Brown."

"Yes. Her name wasn't Miss Brown. She'd come from a rich family in Rhode Island.

She was like an evangelist. She never shouted, never humiliated us."

"Just like you," I said.

"Not at all, Jonah. She didn't have Music and Arters. She had prairie kids, with dirt in their eyes and ears."

"But she got you out of the hardscrabble," Merle said. "She saved your life."

"I'm not so sure about that," Mr. Merriman said. "I think my soul is still on that prairie floor somewhere. But you can't imagine how much I loved Chicago, with a high school right on campus, and a stipend that paid all my bills. I could even send home a little money now and then. I had a lot of friends. I fell in love with a local girl. I read like a fiend. I lived in a dorm. It was my sanctuary, piled with books. I could have gone home during the summer break, but I attended summer school. I was voracious. I graduated in three years. I didn't stay in Chicago. I had a scholarship to Columbia."

I was curious about his romance. "What happened to the local girl?"

"Oh, she stayed in Chicago. We were much too young. We kept in touch. She married a pharmacist in Oak Park."

That name struck a bolt in my head. "Isn't that where Hemingway is from?"

Papa Hemingway, as he liked to call himself, would go on to win the Nobel Prize. We'd studied Papa's stories in Mr. Merriman's class. Merriman had told us that the space between Papa's sentences was as important as the sentences themselves. That space served as an island, he said, and each sentence had its own separate story to tell. I remember hearing a news report on the radio this past January that Papa and his fourth wife, Mary, had died in a plane crash in East Africa, along the upper Nile. There was a ton of obituaries, with his grey beard on the cover of every newspaper. We came to Merriman's class with candles and lit them in homage to Papa and his wife. "It's the early Hemingway I mourn," Merriman had said. "The Hemingway of Paris who sat in a coffeehouse on the Place Contrescarpe and wrote his short stories in blue notebooks, wearing a sweatshirt to keep himself warm. I don't mourn the clown he became—the bullfighter, the civilian soldier with his own private army, who lost that precious island between each sentence. And all he was left with was an empty song."

And then the obituaries vanished, as Papa and his wife were found with a few broken ribs.

Merle scolded Mr. Merriman in class. "You're too harsh. Fame distorts. Fame followed him wherever he went. Celebrate the writer he once was, when he was undiscovered, and sat alone in his sweatshirt, with icicles in the window."

Merriman couldn't answer Merle. No one could . . .

THE ARTICLE ON Merriman was a sensation. It was mostly Merle's doing. The dean loved it and so did the Parents Association. We had our usual byline, but Phyllis received most of the credit. We didn't care. We'd written about a teacher we adored, a teacher who was concerned about us the way Miss Brown was concerned about Jonathan in Mr. Merriman's lost novel. But our elation didn't last.

Merle began to fall, even with her cane and the anchor of her brace. The doctors who examined her couldn't find the cause. The muscles of her leg weren't flaccid. And the leg brace should have increased her mobility. But she would suddenly crumple to the ground. So far, the falls hadn't been serious. But David had to pull her out of class until he could resolve the mystery of Merle's falls, although Merle herself wanted to stay at Music and Art.

Suddenly, without any apparent reason, the bones in her

other leg grew brittle. Merle began to use a wheelchair. She called it her chariot. But she didn't want to ride the halls of the Castle on wheels. "Jonah," she said, "I'm not even sure the Board of Education would allow it. M & A doesn't have a single ramp."

David hired a horde of tutors. But they couldn't keep up with her intelligence. They all quit. Professors came from Columbia. Merle was feisty with them. They all quit, too. It was only Mr. Merriman who could soften her anger and despair. He wouldn't accept money from David. He sat with Merle once or twice a week, would arrive around six. She had him to herself for three hours. I never interfered.

Merle would ride her chariot to the dinner table promptly at nine. I was often invited, too. Flora sat with us, flirting with Mr. Merriman. Alice Messenger was much less morose and had gone back to preparing the family dinners. She liked having Mr. Merriman around.

I think David was a bit jealous of him and the hold he had on Merle. "You're a farm boy, aren't you, Mr. Merriman?"

"David, I'm not conducting a class. I'm Tom at the dinner table. Yes, I grew up on a farm. I loved my mother and father, but we were never close. I had to attend to my little brothers. The soil was poor on the prairie. The wind blew it everywhere. The grit was in our soup, in our hair, in our eyelids. It left you blind during a sand storm. I was never much of a farmer, David. The prairie was used to silence. I was used to words. But I'm still a farm boy. Whatever language I have came from those long silences."

I listened. I'd never had sand in my eyes, but I wasn't so different from Merriman. We'd both traveled very far. He'd gone from the prairie to Chicago and New York. I'd gone from Minford Place to Music and Art.

FIFTEEN

War

WITHOUT A SINGLE warning, the Webster Avenue Cannibals crossed Crotona Park and invaded our territory. Not only that, the Cannibals went deep into the terrain that belonged to the Black Barons of Boston Road. Attacking two gangs at once was either an act of folly or a bold maneuver. Webster Avenue wanted to occupy an entire swath of the South Bronx and become the lords of the largest lair that any street gang had ever held, at least in my memory. They entered shops and markets at will and stole whatever merchandise that pleased them. They drew their insignia—a white skull with black eyeholes—on the stoops of apartment houses and on the signboards of tailor shops. Not only that, they carried zip guns carved out of wood, with primitive barrels and rubber bands used as firing pins. All the gangs had zip guns designed by their most ingenious members. But they were meant for show. Zip guns were never used in battle—that was Bronx etiquette. And here were the Cannibals with their zips.

They marched into our clubhouse and immediately took

command, declaring the Wolves and Wolverines they met smooching on the gang's disheveled couches as prisoners of war, and then releasing them, since they didn't want to get arrested on a kidnapping rap. But the Cannibals tore our clubhouse apart, painted white skulls everywhere, and wrote on the ceiling:

A WARNING FROM WEBSTER AVENUE
DISAPPEAR OR DIE

They shot out the lights of several lampposts with their zips and left a note at the kosher butcher shop on Southern Boulevard. The note was for me:

> *Jonah Salt, listen to us.*
> *Your great tactician is gone.*
> *Michael Salt is condemned to Castle Billy.*
> *He will never return to Minford Place.*
> *You have a gang of losers and misfits with their Wolverines.*
> *Either the remains of your gang become a branch of Webster Avenue,*
> *Or we will wipe you out.*
> *Reconsider.*
> *The choice is yours.*
> *The Cannibals are ready for a meet.*

I wasn't a warlord. I was Michael's baby brother, a baby brother with biceps. I could draw silver wolves and dead people for a funeral parlor, but I had no master plan. Our midnight patrols were a miserable failure. Webster Avenue had walked right in.

The Cannibals had white paint on their faces like Batman's arch enemy, Joker. But they never wore Joker's sinister smile. They looked like skeletons in street clothes, skeletons that could dash about and shoot at lampposts with their zips. All of Minford Place was frightened of skeletons in the neighborhood.

I had no choice. I skipped school and went to Castle Billy. Michael didn't bother to read the Cannibals' note.

"It was bound to happen, kid. The Wolves let down their guard. And the Cannibals saw their opportunity. They shouldn't have messed with the Black Barons. That was their big mistake. Seize one territory at a time. That's always been the rule."

"What are our options, big brother?"

Michael looked at me with his own skeletal face. I could see the bones behind the skin. "You have none," he said.

"Couldn't we join up with the Barons and counterattack?"

Michael grimaced and I could catch a glimpse of his blood-red gums. "It would end in a slaughter, kid. I told you to be vigilant, to protect your home ground. The cops are on their side now."

"Why?" I asked. "Why?"

"Because the Cannibals are too damn big. Did you know that their headquarters and Captain Shelly's precinct are a few blocks apart?"

"So they're blood brothers," I said, "the Cannibals and the cops."

Michael wouldn't answer. A military policeman unchained his leg from his chair and escorted Michael back to his cell.

I didn't have to rush to the docks. The ferry sat right

there, with its roof at a slant. I paid my nickel and climbed aboard.

I had a visitor waiting for me at South Street. It was Captain Shelly. He wasn't wearing his gold-braided jacket. He'd come to me in his civvies again, almost like a spy.

"Jonah, do you want to stay out of jail? Children's Court would love to hear from you. I gave you a chance. I told you to watch your perimeters. Now you'll have to fold your tent and come to terms with the Cannibals."

I watched the way his mouth moved like a moist machine. His eyebrows reminded me of dead trees, that's how bald they were.

"Cap, do I have a choice?"

"No."

And he left me there at the docks.

I WASN'T A strategist like Michael, but I had to think like one. I brought a white bandanna, attached it to a stick, and stood at the border of the Black Barons terrain on Boston Road. I didn't have long to wait. Alvin James arrived. Both of us took pride in the 1954 World Series. Cleveland was the heavy favorite to beat the hell out of Willie and the Giants. They had the hitting and the pitching and had won 111 games during the regular season. But Willie tore the heart out of Cleveland in the first game of the series with a spectacular catch of a long line drive to centerfield, running with his back to the ball, as if he had radar in the webbing of his glove. He plucked that ball out of the air like a miracle man.

"Home boy, what happened to the glove I got you?"

I lied. "I lost it, Alvin."

"Ain't no matter. I'll get you another."

Then we talked about the chalk-faced Cannibals, how that gang had raided our territories, and what we ought to do about it.

I went to the Wolves' war council. I didn't find much eagerness to grapple with the Cannibals. But I did have four members on my side. And we worked out a plan with Alvin and the Barons.

The next time those chalk faces appeared with their zip guns to terrorize us, we rushed out of an alley—four Wolves and four Barons—and whacked the zips out of their hands, the Willie Way, with baseball bats. It wasn't much of a rumble. But the cops arrived out of nowhere, a dozen of them, seized our war trophies, and arrested us. We rode to the 48th precinct in handcuffs, were fingerprinted, and sat in detention cells. Some of us were sent to the Juvenile Division, while others, who were older, went straight to Criminal Court.

Luckily, I was with Alvin James. Lawyers sat around and represented us. They all had a crack in their faces that served as a smile. I knew the grift. If I didn't cop a plea, I would sit around for months and months in juvenile jail before I was called back into court. The judge looked at my record a long time. She must have been forty-five or fifty. She had a wrinkled robe and a curl over one eye.

"Young man," she said, "what are you doing here? I have a daughter at Music and Art."

She sentenced me to sixty days.

I WAS A JUVIE all over again. I even had my old cell. The same cliques congregated out in the yard. I wasn't harmed.

There were half a dozen Cannibals in their white paint. The guards didn't bother about me, and the chalk faces left me alone. I hung out with Alvin James and his crew. There were as many Barons as Cannibals this year.

I called my mom. "Anita, don't bother to come. Spofford is my favorite hotel."

David showed up the next day. He was annoyed. "Christ, why didn't you call from the precinct? I would have had my own lawyer on the case. You wouldn't be sitting here now."

David didn't know a damn thing about Juvenile Justice. His hot-shot lawyer would have gotten me a stiffer sentence. I learned a lot talking to other juvies on my first trip to Spofford. The judges were much tougher if a juvie's lawyer opted for a trial. There was all this additional expense and the judge made a juvie pay for it with a longer sit at Spofford. So I took my sixty days.

But David had already talked to the judge. And he convinced her to let me go to school during my detention. So a bus picked me up at seven AM and drove me and four other juvies to different junior and senior high schools in Manhattan and the Bronx. We wore handcuffs on the bus. And the guard from Spofford made a show of unshackling me right in front of the Castle. That bastard loved to belittle us. I'm sure I was the first juvie M & A ever had and probably the last.

Mr. Merriman was nice about it, but the other kids in my journalism class looked at me like I was a piece of dirt. Dean Amanda called me into her office.

"I made this exception for you, Jonah. I could have denied you entrance into our Castle.

It's an ugly sight to see a boy in handcuffs right outside

the front door. It leaves a bad taste in the mouth. I am putting you on notice. If there is the slightest chicanery, you will be dismissed from Music and Art. Is that clear, young man?"

Amanda should have been kinder to me. The articles Merle and I had done in *Overtone* had given the school some pizzazz, as the admen liked to say at David's shop. But I was a juvie, and a juvie had no rights.

I sat alone in the lunchroom.

Phyllis Pearl didn't shun me. She slid her lunch tray next to mine.

"I'd ask you to write about your experiences at Spofford," she said, "but Amanda would never allow it to be printed. She'd disband the entire editorial staff. She doesn't want you advertised, advertised at all. But you could still help me edit other articles. I would welcome that."

So I worked with the cubbies, taught them what to slice out of a sentence and what to keep. I was a member of *Overtone*'s editorial board, the boy with the red pencil. Phyllis brought me to conferences with the dean.

Amanda blew her nose in front of us. "Phyllis, why is *he* here?" she asked, pointing the blade of her letter opener at me.

"Jonah is essential," Phyllis said. "I couldn't edit *Overtone* without him."

"Fine," Amanda said, "but I don't need to see his face. I should have left him to rot in that jail."

I'd had enough of Amanda. "Why didn't you, Ma'am?"

She started to cackle. "And have a rebellion on my hands? I've never had such a prima donna as *Overtone*'s editor-in-chief."

WE STILL HAD the same pair of misfits who looked after us, Assistant Warden Henshaw, the ex-hockey pro in charge of our cellblock and Matron Millie, the weightlifting champ who wandered around the facility cuffing kids. I kept as far as I could from both of them. But it didn't always work. You could hear one of Millie's moans a mile away. That didn't mean you always had the chance to avoid a cuff on the ear or a swat in the head. Millie had cuffed me several times. And my ear would ring for days. One afternoon I found her writhing on the ground near the volleyball net. She had one of her colossal headaches that nearly blinded Millie and left her helpless.

I could see the enormous size of her calf muscles as they quivered in her tangled skirts. Her shoelaces were untied. I stooped over and tied them. She stared at me with her bloodshot eyes, and Millie motioned with her thick fingers as she continued to writhe on the ground.

"Water," she whispered.

I noticed a crushed paper cup near the water fountain. I uncrushed it and filled the cup with water. Then I returned to Millie and fed her a few sips.

She grabbed my free hand. The writhing stopped. She squeezed and nearly broke my knuckles.

"Jonah Salt, are you my friend?"

"Yes, Millie."

"Then you won't tell the warden what you just saw?"

"Why should I, Millie?"

"Tell me a story," she said. "I'll get up later on when my head stops swimming."

I smiled to myself. Millie couldn't have known that I was a terrific storyteller.

"What kind of story would you like?"

"An action story," she answered. "And I don't want to hear about the stinking Cannibals." She paused for a second to brush her lips with the back of her hand. "Make it magical."

I didn't have to waver. I told her the story of the wounded wolf that showed up on Longfellow Avenue, and how Michael had tamed that wolf with soap and water, a cup of cottage cheese, and slices of salami.

Millie was in a trance. "The wolf turned to silver in your brother's hands? And she caressed him with her paw?"

"Millie, it might not have been a caress."

She frowned at me. "Don't ruin our story, kid. A caress is a caress."

I didn't have a spot of trouble at Spofford after that incident near the volleyball net. Millie was my protector now. If the Cannibals surrounded me in the yard, their white war paint shimmering in the sun, Millie would rush over and swat them with her huge hands. One of the Cannibals landed in the infirmary. He was clever enough not to lodge a complaint. Millie would have pummeled the entire brotherhood of Cannibals in the clink and Henshaw wouldn't have cared. He despised every single juvie at his jail. He called us "vermin" and "trash" to our faces.

I didn't have any chores to do. Millie scratched me off the list. So I borrowed a book from the jail library. Mr. Merriman had recommended *Ethan Frome*, and it was by a very rich lady, Edith Wharton, who had lived in Europe and won a lot of prizes. I sat in my cell and turned the pages. It was the saddest story I had ever read. The novel took place in a mountain village in Vermont. Ethan Frome, who walked with a noticeable limp, would arrive at the post office promptly at noon, looking for mail that never came. He'd been in love with Mattie, a lady who wasn't his wife. Ethan didn't have the nerve to run off with Mattie. Both of them decided they would rather die than live apart. So they took what they thought would be the last sleigh ride of their lives down a mountain, expecting to crash into a tree. They did crash, but both of them survived. And now Ethan and Mattie, both permanently disabled, lived together, looked after by Ethan's wife.

"The starkness of the prose is the real story," Mr. Merriman had said. "We're on that sleigh ride with Ethan. The book leaves us all slightly awestricken."

I knew I wouldn't forget Ethan Frome. I've never been to Vermont. I've never been anywhere except Governors Island, Creedmoor, and Castle Billy. But I remembered the name of Ethan's village in Vermont—Starkfield. That's the way I felt sometimes, like a stark field in the middle of nowhere. I'd lost my home at Music and Art. I wasn't much more than Phyllis'- red pencil. Merriman couldn't do much. Dean Amanda wasn't on my side.

But I did have a bonus. Merle came to visit in her chariot. David had driven her to Spofford, but he knew that his daughter wanted some time alone with "the convict," as she liked to tease me on the telephone.

She wheeled herself around like a marathon racer. The other boys at Spofford were jealous that I had a girl of my own.

"I miss you, Jonah," she said, "I miss you a lot."

Her dark eyes stood out in the starkness of the visitors' room. We couldn't hold hands. We couldn't kiss. I told her how much I liked *Ethan Frome*.

"Oh, I read that book when I was a child," she said. "One of my teachers in grammar school was a grandniece of the author. I have a signed copy at home. I've read all her books."

"Did you like *Ethan Frome*?"

"I loved it, Jonah. Ethan was such a tragic figure and he had no way of expressing his tragedy, no way but his limp."

I remembered the snow and the sleigh ride. I'd never seen mountain snow. And I wondered if Michael's wolf had come from Vermont. In my mind, it loped along the streets of Starkfield, looking for kinship and finding none.

I COULDN'T FIND any kinship of my own. Henshaw had Millie transferred to another cellblock. And then the Black Barons were released, one by one. The three other Wolves who had been arrested with me weren't juveniles and probably sat at Rikers right now. I sat alone. The chalk faces in the yard smiled like jackals. I couldn't appeal to Henshaw. He wasn't interested in my fate. I turned to my patroness at the Belevedere, Rosalind Silverstein, who ran her late husband's funeral parlor and preferred to drink her Lipton's out of a metal tea holder. But she couldn't be found, either at the mortuary or the cafeteria. I called Milton, the Belevedere's manager, from the pay phone at Spofford. I had to wait in line for an hour with my handful of nickels.

"Ah, the young artist," Milton said. "We miss your company. Mrs. Silverstein hasn't been a guest lately. We've stocked up on strawberry shortcake and our entire supply has gone stale."

"But I called her at the funeral parlor and the phone keeps ringing. Nobody picks up."

"There's been an unfortunate accident," Milton said. "The funeral parlor was firebombed and Madame Silverstein disappeared with the fire. We've had our own misfortunes. Some young scamps painted white skulls all over our windows. Cannibals they call themselves. And the moment we scrape those horrid skulls off, an entire field of skulls come back. Jonah, we're window blind. We can't tell whether it's night or day at the Belevedere. I'd like to hire you to get rid of those scamps and their skulls. Name your price."

"Milton," I said, "I can't do much from a jail cell."

"Then you're no longer of much use to us at the Belevedere," he said and hung up.

I'd lost every protector I had at Spofford. Alvin James and the Barons were gone, and Millie was in another cellblock. I was all alone, like my brother's silver wolf. And then things got worse. I checked the new arrivals. One of the chalk faces was assigned to the next cell. I recognized him right away under his war paint. Percival Good, the president and chief enforcer of the Cannibals.

What the hell was he doing here? Percival wasn't a juvie. He must have been nineteen. Had someone planted him here? Or had Rikers suddenly become much too crowded, and Spofford was used as an overspill? Whatever the reason, it stank worse than a juvie's sour sweat.

Let me tell you about Percival Good. He wasn't a bodybuilder like Michael and me. Percival wasn't muscular at all. He was lean and very long. His knuckles were like razor blades. He was as fast on his feet as Sugar Ray Robinson, the middleweight champion of the world, who lived in the North Bronx, near Kingsbridge Avenue. Sugar Ray drove around in a pink Cadillac. He often tossed candy out of his car to kids in the neighborhood. And Percival was known as the South Bronx's Sugar Ray. He never fought in the ring. But he took on all challengers in Crotona Park. The park itself was neutral territory. All the gangs could parade in their colors. I watched Percival in his bare-knuckle fights. Bruisers came from Cincinnati and Detroit to battle the king of Crotona Park. The purse was a hundred bucks, put up by the Cannibals themselves. But no one ever grabbed that purse from *our* Sugar Ray.

I never missed a single one of his matches. They had become part of our local lore. Percival didn't charge any admission. He liked having huge crowds. And he made a fortune on side bets. Some of his opponents were professionals. It didn't really matter who they were or what record they had in the ring. They couldn't keep up with Percival in Crotona Park.

A circle was drawn by one of the Cannibals with white chalk. Only the two fighters could step inside that circle. We all stood outside the chalk marks in a great big crowd that covered half the plains and hills of Crotona Park. And if one of the fighters was knocked outside the circle, we shoved him back in, no matter if it was Percival or his opponent.

I saw the blood. I didn't wince. None of his opponents could dance the way Percival danced. He could take a punch. He would spit out a tooth and laugh. He'd bob and weave in that mask of white paint and then the jabs would come like licks of lightning.

There were no rounds or limits or a bell keeper. We didn't have any bells or a referee.

None of the professional fighters could last more than a minute or two against Percival's lightning blows. They didn't have Percival's knuckles. They were used to wearing padded gloves. I didn't care if he was a Cannibal or not. Percival

Good was a hero of mine. And he occupied the next cell at Spofford. Somebody close to the Cannibals had put him in the clink to knock my brains out with his bare knuckles.

Percival didn't threaten me. He didn't have to. His mere presence was a threat. He sat down next to me in the mess hall.

"Jonah Salt," he said in the quiet voice of a choir boy, "I've seen you at my fights. You never rooted for the other guy. And I'm a Cannibal."

"Come on, Percival. You're our Sugar Ray."

I'd swear that the Cannibals' enforcer blushed. "Aw, I don't have Sugar's moves. I wouldn't last a round with Sugar Ray."

"What about a bare-knuckle fight?"

Percival didn't even have to ponder. "Jonah, he'd knock me right into Indian Lake with or without a glove."

Indian Lake was the one bit of countryside we had in the South Bronx. Young couples would come there with baby carriages. No one interfered with them. Old men would play cards on milk boxes in the light of the moon. The lake was almost like a summer resort. And north of the lake was Indian Rock, a sunbather's paradise. My mother and father met on that rock, while both were sunbathing. But that had little to do with Percival and my predicament.

"Take a guess why I'm here, Jonah?"

I didn't have to guess. "You'll see to it that I leave Spofford without a head."

Percival laughed. "I wouldn't touch a thinker like you. I got myself invited into Spofford to make sure that no one else interferes when the other Cannibals tear off your flesh."

I kept away from the shower stalls. I timed my hours at the mess when the guards and the nurses were at the tables. I needed witnesses, other eyes and ears. But I was lost in the folly of words after I read *Ethan Frome* for the eleventh time, and like a fool I ventured out into the yard. It was full of juvies in their mackinaw jackets. Suddenly they disappeared, as if someone had signaled to them. That someone was Percival. He stood there with his brotherhood of Cannibals.

"Jonah," he said in that soft voice of his, "let's call a truce. You'll leave this yard alive, but we need a bit of compensation. What about if we broke your arms and left you with one good eye? You could still go back to school. And you might even graduate. You'd have to wear an eye patch like Henshaw."

I wasn't as brave as Michael. I liked having the luxury of two eyes. I was about to crap in my pants until I saw Matron Millie at the other end of the yard. She was taking a shortcut between two cellblocks when she recognized me and the Cannibals. She marched right over.

"Percival Good," she said, "is that you?"

He'd been here before, maybe several times. Webster Avenue's Sugar Ray must have honed his knuckles at Spofford on other juvies.

"Yes, Ma'am," he said in that polite voice of his. Percival was always polite, even when he cut you to pieces with those razor-sharp knuckles.

"And are you meaning to do Jonah harm?"

Percival didn't stall, he never did. "I'd be lying, Ma'am, if I said I ain't."

"Well, I can't allow that," she said. "And it has nothing to do with this facility and its rules. Jonah came to my assistance when I had one of my blinders. And I'd be a rotten skunk if I didn't help him now."

Percival pleaded with her. "But there are five of us, Miss Millie."

"Wouldn't matter if there were ten," she told him.

I could see that he was fond of Millie, that he genuinely liked her. Maybe she was kind to him on his previous stays at Spofford. He must have fought the entire jail, and she attended to him in the infirmary.

"Tell you what, Miss Millie. I'll leave the other Cannibals out of this rumble."

Millie stared at him with her mournful eyes. "It's not a rumble, Percy. It's a conversation that gets quick."

As much as he liked Millie, Percival didn't waste any time. He jabbed at her with those razor blades of his. In less than a minute her face was marked with blood. But he was merciful with Millie. He didn't dance, didn't have the usual lightning in his fists, the lightning I had seen in Crotona Park. His blows were more measured. He didn't want to hurt her more than he had to. But she wouldn't back away from his blows. She didn't protect her face. Millie stood her ground.

Blood flew from her lips. But it didn't seem to matter how often his blows landed, or how many cuts she had on her face. She didn't lose her balance. She didn't fall. Percival exhausted himself. He lost his wind. Millie captured his fists in her hands, and I listened to Percival squeal. She cracked all his knuckles, broke his wrists. None of the other Cannibals jumped on Millie. They stood there, stupefied, as Percival fainted and fell to the ground.

Millie scooped him up in her arms and carried him to the infirmary.

SIXTEEN

Boundaries

I VISITED WEBSTER Avenue's enforcer. Both his hands were encased in plaster. They looked like big vanilla boxing gloves. He played the clown, pretending to take big bites out of his vanilla gloves. There was nothing personal about his malice, even if he'd been let into Spofford to help his brother Cannibals disable me, so I couldn't revive the Wolves. I learned a lot about him as he sat in bed. He'd trained so hard for his bare-knuckle bouts, he never had time for school. The truant officers came after Percival again and again. He'd discovered reading at the Spofford library during his first detention. He could manage a page or two, but not much more than that. So I didn't have a choice. I read *Ethan Frome* to him in its entirety. I was a truant that day. I didn't get on the Spofford bus to Music and Art.

I couldn't tell whether Percival was touched by Ethan's sad tale.

"Read it again," he barked after I got to the last page. "I couldn't catch all the words."

I didn't have the breath for another marathon like that. "Percival, what did you think of Ethan?"

"I liked his long silences."

I was released from confinement the very next day. Millie said goodbye to me in the mess hall, her cuts covered with bandages and cotton wool. She looked like a medieval soldier, or what I imagined a medieval soldier to be.

"It's your last stay, Jonah. You'll end up at Rikers the next time around. And I won't be

there to protect you."

She stroked my cheek in front of the whole mess hall.

I walked home. I was in hostile territory. The chalk faces occupied our clubhouse with

their white skulls on the walls—more than half the Wolverines had gone over to their side. I couldn't find any of the Silver Wolves. They must have been in hiding.

I went to the Belevedere. The window was still covered with white skulls. Milton sulked when he saw me. But he didn't keep me out of the cafeteria. It was filled with Cannibals. They wore their colors. I couldn't wear mine. I asked Milton about the Widow.

Milton barely looked at me. "I believe the Widow's dead."

"What makes you think that?"

"Ah," Milton answered with absolute coldness, "she couldn't survive without her strawberry shortcake and her Lipton's in a Russian tea holder."

It was clear. He blamed me and the rest of my gang for the Cannibals' invasion of his cafeteria. The Silver Wolves had lost their sense of boundaries. He wasn't wrong. We'd let the bastards in. None of their members caused a commotion. But the Belevedere had little gaiety with chalk faces around. Milton didn't lose any customers. They had nowhere else to go. But the poets were a little quieter in their corner of the cafeteria. The ladies in their knitting circle no longer laughed. The retired stockbrokers whispered to themselves about their colossal losses and gains.

The Silver Wolves no longer had their own separate table. And I didn't see Michael's lieutenant, Dave Barber. The Belevedere must have hired a new captain of the busboys. But I was stubborn. I found a spot at our old table and sat there with my sketch pad. I knew those bandits with their chalk faces had planned to blind me in one eye and had connived to get their enforcer inside Spofford to accomplish that mission. But they ignored me at the Belevedere, as if Jonah Salt did not exist. It's possible that Percival himself had a change of heart after I recited *Ethan Frome* to him. I didn't care. I sketched the chalk faces as they strutted about the cafeteria. They were little more than skeletons on my sketch pad. They wandered over to my table and stared at my designs, pretending not to recognize me.

"Hey, you got masterpieces. Can we buy some of your art, kid?"

I tore the pages out of my pad and thrust them at the Cannibals.

"You can have them for free."

I WENT SHOPPING at the supermarket and prepared scrambled eggs and a sardine salad for Mom as a midnight snack. She looked tired when she came through the door, the key trembling in her fist. Mom seemed surprised to see me.

"You pirate," she said. "You should have told me you were getting out of jail."

"Anita," I said, "Spofford isn't a jail. It's a rest home for juvies. Have you noticed a difference in the streets?"

Her brow rippled. "What difference?"

"The Cannibals have conquered our territory."

"You mean the boys with white paint? They're very polite. They escorted me home from the factory."

"That's not the point, Anita. They don't belong here."

And we sat down to eat. She savored the scrambled eggs and the sardine salad. "It seems we have a chef in the family."

I was still annoyed. "Mom, we're prisoners of war."

I returned to Music and Art the next day. It was the first time in two months I hadn't come in handcuffs. I didn't belong anywhere. I was just a juvie on vacation. Mr. Merriman could see how fragile I was. Phyllis Pearl was out with the flu, so Merriman made me acting editor-in-chief. I worked with the cubs and *Overtone*'s other editors. I put all the articles in their proper place. The lead was an interview with Oscar Ramirez, a businessman from the South Bronx who served as the lone maverick on the Board of Education. Ramirez wanted free lunches for every student in the city school system. He wanted the city to hire thousands of tutors and to provide shelter for every homeless student.

"Children cannot learn under duress," he told Phyllis in the interview. "They cannot live in the land of chaos."

I took the layout of the next issue to the dean. Amanda

wasn't happy to find me in Phyllis' place. "I see you're back from juvenile jail. Jonah, that's good. Half the school won't have to see you in handcuffs."

She looked at the layout and was furious. "Ramirez is a radical. We can't print that interview on the front page. Bury it somewhere."

"But he's on the Board of Ed. He has the right to his own opinion."

"Bury it."

I did. I put the article on the last page. But I delayed sending the layout to the printer until Phyllis returned. Now she was the furious one. Phyllis restored the original layout, and Dean Amanda simply canceled the issue out of spite. Phyllis fought back. She had Student Affairs invite Oscar Ramirez as a guest speaker at M & A.

We all assembled in the auditorium to hear him. I'd read the interview. He'd come off the streets to start a construction company that was worth millions. He worked alongside his own men. He also bought up abandoned tenements at city auctions, rebuilt them, and charged a reasonable rent. He set up soup kitchens in the poorest neighborhoods. He sang in his church choir. He was the wealthiest man on the Board of Education, and as Amanda said, the most radical.

Amanda herself introduced him. Ramirez was very tall. He labored hard on construction sites, and I imagined his muscles rippling under his herringbone suit. He didn't hesitate when he spoke to us. Oscar Ramirez gripped the sides of the podium with his huge hands.

"Boys and girls, I'm a bum."

A couple of students snickered, but I was riveted to my chair.

"I could never have gotten into a school like Music and Art," he said. "I didn't have the talent or the grades. And I regret what I missed. It's an anomaly. I'm the only member of the Board of Ed without an education." He nearly tore the podium to pieces with his grip, that's how riled up he was. "I don't want to see students suffer the way I suffered. I asked the Board to hire five thousand tutors and place them in various schools. Board members laughed at me. 'Oscar's delusional,' they said. 'He'll sink the whole system. We already have remedial classes. We don't have the budget for five thousand extra tutors.' I offered to pay for some of them myself. They threw up other obstacles. 'How would we certify Oscar's little army of tutors?' The whole idea was scratched. And I wondered to myself. What if there's a kid out there who can't handle the academic stuff, and what if there are thousands like him—or her? They'll crash dive. And we'll never save them. I was in a remedial class. I learned nothing. We were called the dummies. Well, I'll see to it that there's no more of that. Education is all we'll ever have. It isn't the city's gift to you. Boys and girls, it's an obligation."

Dean Amanda revived the issue with Oscar's interview in it. She was photographed with Oscar on the front page. That article was the envy of every high school paper. Editors congratulated us. Phyllis wasn't satisfied. She wanted to plunge deeper and deeper into whatever inequality she could find. I had other worries—the presence of chalk faces on our streets. The Cannibals moved about with their insignias and colors, and their sense of privilege and domination. But they didn't have the same success with the Boston Road Barons. Wilkins Avenue was the dividing line; the

Black Barons flourished south of Wilkins, and the Wolves had the north until the chalk faces stole our territory.

It was different on the Barons' side of the line. Grandmas threw bags of garbage down on the Cannibals from their windowsills. The librarians at the public library's Morrisania branch wouldn't allow the Cannibals to paint white skulls near the bookshelves. They stood their ground against the chalk faces. These librarians were much braver than the Belevedere, a cafeteria that capitulated to the Cannibals. And Alvin James was a much smarter warlord than the Wolves ever had, except for Michael himself. He put up barricades of broken pushcarts whenever the Cannibals appeared and hurled hot tar at them with slingshots. The Cannibals had to give up the struggle after their first invasions failed. They had much easier pickings north of the divide.

It troubled me. I saw them in the market on Jennings Street, stealing charlotte russes from the Russian bakery, licking off the custard and whipped cream like vultures. I saw them dance around young girls and frighten them with their war paint. I saw them shove old men aside and overturn a Bungalow Bar ice cream wagon. I saw them sit at the soda fountain near Seabury Place with our Wolverines and rifle through the comic book racks. I saw them feed themselves on Batman and Joker.

I wanted them out of the Wolves' lost terrain. I went looking for our gang members,

trying to muster them, but I couldn't recruit a single one. And that's when Percival reappeared. He must have discovered an escape route out of Spofford. He still wore plaster on his mitts, his vanilla gloves, and he wore the Cannibals' colors on his back—light grey and blood red.

"Jonah," he muttered in that soft voice of his, "stop your search. I had to convince our war council that you were harmless. But now I'm not so sure. You'll be followed, kid, wherever you go. You don't want to end up like Ethan Frome. And we know where your mother works—at the chocolate factory."

I was mad as hell. "Leave my mother out of this, Percival."

"Can't, kid. War is war."

SO I HAD to get up at six and escort my mom to the chocolate factory and bring her home near midnight. Those vultures in war paint followed behind us and whistled at my mom.

"Mrs. Salt, Mrs. Salt, can we help you dip the cherry into the chocolate?"

I wanted to go after the Cannibals, but Mom grabbed my arm.

"Ignore them, Jonah," she said, and swatted at one of the Cannibals with her umbrella. I realized I wasn't protecting Mom. Mom was protecting me.

But I couldn't do anything about the vultures during her lunch hour, when she usually went shopping at Jennings Street. I was at M & A. Merriman noticed how rattled I was. I told him about the Cannibals. He said one word.

"Oscar."

I was confused. Oscar Ramirez was on the Board of Ed. But then I remembered how he had made his millions. After class, I went to one of his construction sites on the Silver Wolves' old terrain near Crotona Park. Ramirez happened to be on site in a metal helmet, like the other men. He didn't recognize me. Actually, we'd never met.

"Music and Art. You spoke there. Five thousand tutors, you said. I'm Jonah Salt."

He could have been one of the Cannibals, that's how much white dust he had on his face. The sleeves of his sweatshirt were rolled up and I could see the sinews on his forearms, and the abundant layers of muscle.

"Hello," he said with an embarrassed smile. "I was a bit carried away. I'm considered a crazy man in some circles."

"You make a lot of sense to me. I wouldn't have minded all those tutors. I might need one for myself."

The smile remained, but his blue eyes lost a little of their luster. "How can I help?"

"Sir, have you noticed any skeletons marching around lately?"

He was much more interested all of a sudden. "Skeletons on Boston Road?"

"Yes. The Cannibals of Webster Avenue are occupying these grounds and they wear white paint on their faces. You must have noticed them."

"I thought they were clowns," Ramirez said.

"They are. Sinister clowns, sir. They'd love to claim the South Bronx for themselves."

"Does Captain Lawrence know about this? He commands—"

"Captain Shelly sent them to us," I said. "They police the area for him, collect criminals. But they're criminals themselves."

Ramirez's blue eyes seemed to rattle in his head. "Wait here."

He returned without his helmet. He wore a blue jacket over his sweatshirt and coveralls. He hadn't changed his dusty workman's boots. He looked like a Bronx cavalier.

He had his Oldsmobile parked near the site. We got into the car, crossed the Third Avenue Bridge into Manhattan and drove down to Police Headquarters on Centre Street with its twin stone lions out front. I wondered if the twins were guarding us or the cops inside the iron door. Oscar parked his Olds, but we didn't go near the lions. We walked into an Italian restaurant across the street. It was full of customers at five in the afternoon. We'd crashed a party. I noticed a banner strung from wall to wall:

**WELCOME TO THE ANNUAL
POLICE CAPTAINS GALA.**

None of the captains wore a uniform. They were dancing with their wives and fiancées, or else they collected around the bar with their fellow officers. There was a band near the bar, a trumpeter, an accordionist, and a piano player. They were much younger than the captains. They might have been members of the Police Academy.

Most of the captains and their wives knew Oscar Ramirez. There was a lot of hugging, and Oscar introduced me as a prodigy from the High School of Music and Art. I wasn't a prodigy. I was a gang member in search of his gang.

We didn't have to wander around looking for Captain Shelly. He spotted us. And he was furious—not at Oscar, but at my appearance at the gala with him. He gave Oscar a bear hug.

"How did you meet this young champion?" he asked Oscar Ramirez.

"I spoke at his school. He came to my Crotona Park site. He told me about the boys from Webster Avenue, how aggressive they have been."

Captain Shelly stared at me as he talked to Oscar. "Aggressive? I would use another word. Vigilant. I know you have a night watchman. But has any machinery been missing from that site? Watchmen love to steal, but they can't with the Cannibals around. I work with them. They take pressure off the police. They're guardians of every neighborhood they secure. Yes, they're a gang, Oscar. But they're under my control. I have the stats. There's much less crime with the Cannibals around."

"But Jonah tells me they are the real criminals."

"Nonsense," the captain said. "They frighten criminals away. Yes, they're a little rough at times. But they're a street gang with their own rituals. And the gang they dismantled, the Silver Wolves, weren't angels either."

Oscar went off to greet several other captains and their wives. And I was stuck with Shelly.

His cheeks were on fire. "You should have left Ramirez out of this. Whatever complaints you had, you could have come to me. My door was never closed to you."

"Cap, the Cannibals wanted to take out one of my eyes."

"That will never happen," he said.

"They've been following my mother around."

"That won't happen again," he said.

He left me standing there. Oscar was having such a good time. He danced with several of the captains' wives. He did the polka, whirling one captain's wife after another to the far ends of the restaurant, while the captains themselves clapped their hands and stamped their feet on the floorboards. Then he drank champagne and toasted every captain at the restaurant. He forgot all about me and why he'd come to the captain's gala. I rode the subway back to the Bronx.

SEVENTEEN

A Sunday Girl

MORE AND MORE Silver Wolves came out of the shadows. I'm not sure who had converted them—Percival or one of his "preachers." But they wore the blood red of the Cannibals. And so did the Wolverines. When I confronted Diana Coleman in her new colors, she snorted at me, "Wake up, Jonah. The Wolves are dead."

Dave Barber got his old job back at the Belevedere now that he was a Cannibal. The clubhouse displayed the new colors. Chalk faces went in and out of that abandoned building with Wolverines in blood red. Michael and I were the last two Silver Wolves alive. And he couldn't wear his colors at Castle Billy. But I wore mine, even when I went to the Jennings Street market with a glass jar for the half-sour pickles that Mom loved. Jake the pickle man didn't have a store or even a stand. He had five barrels—three for pickles, one for sauerkraut, and one for pickled herring. He'd become a myth in the South Bronx. Millionaires from all five boroughs would have their chauffeurs drive to Jennings Street with glass jars to pick up a week's supply of pickles.

Jake was as rough with them as he was with me. He looked like a vagabond. He wore an apron that was never washed. He had a flannel shirt with a missing sleeve. His pants had holes in them. That was his uniform on Jennings Street. He kept an enormous wallet around his waist, stuffed with coins and dollar bills. No one had ever dared make off with his treasure. He was Captain Shelly's favorite pickle man, even though there were half a dozen pickle stands with assorted barrels at the Bathgate Avenue outdoor market, right next to his precinct.

A patrol car would always arrive from the 48th with pickle jars for Captain Shelly. The patrolman would pay the pickle man and return to Bathgate Avenue, while one or two Cannibals guarded Jake's barrels.

He liked my mother. "Where's Anita?" he asked in his Russian accent. He'd known her for years, before she married my father and had to work two shifts for the family to survive. He'd come out of Siberia as a little boy and first occupied his spot at the market when he was fifteen. He's been here ever since, fighting off other pickle men who wanted his location and his brine.

Anita would come to the market almost every day while Pop was still a car mechanic. She baked cinnamon cookies for the pickle man. He would always save one half-sour pickle for her, the best of his crop. He wasn't that nice to me. He figured it was my fault that Mom had stopped visiting his barrels more than once a week. He was in love with my mother.

"Gangster, can't you send Anita to me?"

"Jake," I said, "she's at the chocolate factory."

"Then you won't get any brine, nothing from the bottom of the barrel."

"That isn't fair."

But he did scoop the bottom of the barrel, did give me the brine. And he wouldn't allow me to pay for the pickles.

"It's for Anita," he said. "It's hard to get through a long afternoon without her coming by."

"Jake, I'll tell her that."

He grew angry. "Gangster, I can tell her myself. I'm a rich man. I'd leave all my barrels, all my brine, to run away with Anita."

"She's married, Jake. Pop wouldn't like that."

The pickle man began to cackle. He had big ears, bigger than mine. "I hear he's in the hospital."

"That doesn't mean she loves him any less."

That night I brought half my bounty of pickles to the Messengers on Central Park West, with a seeded rye bread from the Russian bakery at the market. Merle was home on a holiday from her boarding school. I'm not even sure it was a holiday. I think she just came down from Connecticut for a couple of days. That's how much she missed us. I missed her, too, but we didn't write many letters or talk on the telephone while she was away. Maybe I reminded her too much of the life she had lost at Music and Art. But here she was, with her big brown eyes.

"Hello, wolf boy."

She wore her hair in a ponytail at the Brewster Academy, a high school for girls with disabilities and astronomical IQs. Her cheeks were as sharp as kitchen knives. She wore lipstick now and nail polish. There was an intensity in the movement of her arms that excited me.

David couldn't stop talking about the half-sour pickles in their brine. "Who is this guy?"

"He has a genius for making pickles. He's so spectacular, David, he has police protection."

"How come I never heard of him?"

"Because you don't travel in the world of sour pickles," I said.

"But I grew up on Charlotte Street, a block from the market. Dammit, I must have amnesia. I don't remember a pickle man. I don't remember Jake."

Alice stared at him. "Darling, that's because you're covered with a blanket called Central Park West."

"No," David insisted. "It's the war. It wiped out half my brain. I lost my childhood somewhere, writing memorandums for General Eisenhower. A scratch of my pencil could determine the fate of a whole battalion. I have shellshock, kids, and I never fired a shot."

I felt that way about the Silver Wolves. I was also in shellshock. I'd lost whatever little country I had to the Cannibals.

Alice loved the bread. "Jonah, I can taste every seed. What is it?"

"Russian rye. You can only get it at one bakery in the Bronx. They have a secret supply of caraway seeds."

Flora shoved the entire loaf into the oven, let it sit for twenty minutes, then cut off several slices with a kitchen knife that looked like a hatchet, put ricotta cheese—a household staple—on every slice, with pieces of tomato, and passed them around as an appetizer. Merle and I sipped red wine from the same glass; that wine had become an addiction for David during his stay as General Eisenhower's scribe in France. I think the wine was called Bordeaux.

I never took my eyes off Merle during dinner. I'm not

even sure what we ate after the rye bread and ricotta. We didn't take part in the after-dinner talk. Merle asked to be excused. "Dad, Jonah and I have passionate things to discuss."

She wheeled herself into her room, unclamped the brace and hopped onto the bed, clutching one of my shoulders.

"I'm a juvie, Jonah. All of Connecticut was my jail. Oh, we did our Shakespeare on stage in our chariots. I was Macbeth and Lady Macbeth, depending on the production. But I missed your company as I spoke every line. Kiss me, you silver wolf. What do I care about honor societies and entrance exams?"

"The Wolves are extinct," I said.

"We'll deal with that later."

We kissed on Merle's bed for a very long time. Her tongue had the taste of a peach. I felt like her prisoner. I didn't want to leave the Majestic or Central Park West.

"I was worried that you might meet somebody up in Connecticut. And that's why you stopped writing."

She tapped my head like a queen punishing her page. "I couldn't write. It made me sad, thinking about your brother at Castle Billy, you mother away from six in the morning to midnight, your father locked up at Creedmoor because a nephew stole from him and destroyed his life, and you in your jacket with the wolf's yellow eyes, sent to jail because your own gang deserted you, and you had to come to M & A in handcuffs. All you had was Phyllis and Merriman, and that wasn't enough."

"What about the telephone?" I asked.

"That was worse. I could feel how alone you were from the tremors in your voice. I'm a coward. I should have run away from the academy and come back to you. But I would have disappointed Dad."

MERLE DELAYED AND delayed her return to boarding school. Alice scolded her in front of me. "You'll lose all the equity you've built at Brewster."

A furrow appeared above Merle's left eye. I'd never seen such a dent in her face before. "Equity, Mom? That's a peculiar word. I have no equity at Brewster, and there's none to be had ."

Alice seemed embarrassed. "Students are catty, and if you disappear, they'll forget that you ever existed. And what about your grades?"

"Mom, my grades will never suffer. You know that. And let them all be catty. What do I care? I have you and Dad and Flora and my dreamboat with his pompadour."

"Merle, I don't have a pompadour," I said in my own defense.

"You did when you first came to M & A. That's how I noticed you. And I asked myself, 'What is this ruthless boy doing at such a tame school?' Don't pout. It was meant as a compliment."

She had a sudden urge to have a picnic in Central Park. Flora prepared sandwiches and a thermos of lemonade. We went down in the elevator with the thermos hanging from a chain around my neck and the sandwiches in the saddlebag of the wheelchair. We crossed into the park. Merle moved at such a quick pace, I had a hard time keeping up with her. I worried that she might crash into a child, but she always managed to swerve.

Then she stopped and we sat on a bench. "Jonah, do you think we'll ever have babies?"

I didn't know how to answer. She was always a moonbeam ahead of my own thoughts. It was that way with Shakespeare, and with everything else.

She'd become a tease in Connecticut. "Oh, I would love to have a baby with a pompadour."

"Merle, I'm not sure many babies are born with pompadours."

She started to panic. I could tell. She didn't want to go back to Brewster.

"I'm sick of archery contests and debates. I don't want to compete with other girls and other schools. I'd rather stay with the boy who lost his pompadour."

We kissed in the middle of Central Park, among the baby carriages and the dog walkers. Was it possible that a passerby could be looking at us with an odd mixture of disdain and pity? I didn't care. For the moment I had Merle.

SHE STAYED AN extra week, and the headmaster wrote to David that if his daughter didn't return to Brewster, he would have to expel her without a refund for her tuition and room and board. I was with her every moment I could spare. David was silent, still the rebel from Charlotte Street. But Alice pawed at her.

"You can't stay, Merle."

But Merle was stubborn. "I want to see Jonah's big brother again before I go back. Michael practically raised him. And they have a silver wolf in common."

"But he's at Castle Billy, darling. It's a military jail. It doesn't have visiting hours for strangers."

"Stranger, you say?" She'd thrown herself back into the jagged landscape of *Hamlet*. "I'm Jonah's secret bride—no, I was his cousin on my last visit."

Alice shook her head. "Merle, stop the melodramatics. I'll drive you and Jonah to South Street."

And she did.

Merle rode across the ferry ramp in her chariot. The captain welcomed us aboard. I was nervous. I didn't know what state Michael was in. Merle could see the circular fort on Governors Island arise from the mist. The ramp was slightly crooked as we got off the ferry and I had to guide the wheelchair or we would have been stuck.

Castle Billy didn't have any ramps. So we collapsed the wheelchair and I carried it and Merle to the guards' station. We had to wait an hour, as usual. We were the only ones in the visitors' room. Castle Billy seemed haunted without any other guests. Michael arrived in chains. He'd developed a slight tremble since the last time I saw him. He was a walking skeleton, like the Cannibals, but without a painted face or much flesh. He was glad to see Merle. I could tell that he would have liked to clutch her hand.

"Brother," I said, "we lost our terrain."

He looked into my eyes. "Kid, we'll talk about that another time."

"Michael, there is no other time. Do we just capitulate? The Wolves disappeared and the Wolverines went over to the other side. And now the Wolves have come back wearing the Cannibals' colors."

He didn't want to discuss gang business in front of Merle. "Another time."

"Captain Shelly betrayed us," I said.

"The Cap did what he had to do. You should have built yourself a wall after the first white skull was painted in a store window. I warned you what would happen. But I made a deal with Percy."

"Percival came to Castle Billy?"

"Yeah," Michael said. "Out of respect. After you had him hospitalized."

"Mikey, I didn't—"

My brother turned away from me. "Lovebirds," he said. "You make the kid happy."

"Too happy," Merle said. "I have to leave him and return to a school in Connecticut. I'm the captain of the volleyball team."

"You'll be back. Can't keep lovebirds apart."

Merle leaned forward. "I wish we could help."

"You already have," Michael said. "The kid doesn't look so gloomy. Your visit means a lot. Dragging yourself all the way to this fort in the middle of nowhere."

"Your brother carried me up the steps."

"Yeah, the kid's Sir Galahad. He just can't run a gang."

Michael knew how to dig the knife. I didn't have a gang to run.

"Shall I write you, Michael?" Merle asked.

"It would be a waste. The guards pour through all the mail. It comes to me with mustard stains. Jonah tells me you're a reader. Perhaps you could make up a list. I'm on good terms with the librarian."

Michael saw how moody I was. "It's not your fault, kid.

Captain Shelly bet on the Cannibals. They had Percy and a dozen generals. It was bound to happen."

The military cops arrived with a mean grin. I had to watch Michael shuffle off. He waved to Merle and saluted me.

I COULDN'T RIDE up to Connecticut with Merle and her folks. I'd already missed several days of school. But she did write me letters. They arrived like pistol shots:

> *My Dearest Sir Galahad,*
> *I was so glad to see your brother again.*
> *Please don't blame him for his bitterness.*
> *He's a general who lost his army,*
> *A general who can't fight back.*
> *He loves you and can't protect you.*
> *His bitterness grows and grows.*
> *I can't wait for the term to end.*
> *I negotiated with Mom and Dad.*
> *I will be your Sunday girl.*
> *Saturdays are impossible because of volleyball practice.*
> *And if I quit the team I will lose my Sunday privileges.*
> *So keep your Sundays clear,*
> *Or I will join the Cannibals and hunt you down.*
> *Volleys of love from the volleyball queen.*

Boys weren't admitted to Brewster. It was the most prestigious private school in the country for disabled girls. It had a hundred acres near Westport. It had a horse farm, an apple orchard, an archery range, tennis courts, blueberry patches, and its own private lake.

That's what Merle had told me. It had a debating society, a Shakespeare club, a theater that charged admission, and a volleyball team that had never lost a match. And it had Merle. She upset the ordinary routine. She'd read more books than most of her teachers, knew more about drama than Brewster's drama coach, and could play any role that was thrown at her, male and female alike. But she had a rage in her, as Michael did. She preferred M & A's Castle on the Hill to Brewster's volleyball team and an archery range.

The school's chauffeur brought her into Manhattan on Saturday nights, and David drove
her back to Connecticut very early on Monday mornings in time to attend her first class. Merle had no family obligations once she arrived on Central Park West. She was my Sunday girl, as she had said. We could have gone to the Frick, spent an afternoon with the Polish Rider, or pondered over the Picassos at the Museum of Modern Art. But she didn't want the high style of
Manhattan. She'd become another silver wolf. She longed for the lowlands of the South Bronx.

On Sunday morning she arrived in David's Cadillac. She had sandwiches and bottled water, a thermos of lemonade and carrot sticks, pumpkin pie and chicken breasts wrapped in tinfoil, all in her saddlebag. We could have had our picnic on Indian Rock in Crotona Park, where Pop and Mom met. But Merle was like a navigator. She wanted to know the complete landscape of where I had lived. First we went to Longfellow Avenue.

"Show me," she said.

"Show you what?"

"Where you and Michael met the wolf, where he scrubbed that animal and found the silver fur."

"Merle," I said, "have a heart. That was eleven years ago."

"Show me!"

I fumbled around and looked for the spot. "Here," I said, "right under the stoop."

She shut her eyes, and petted the wolf she imagined in her mind. Her strokes were soft and slow, as if she were touching silk.

"Merle," I said, "you can't pet a wolf like that. She's wild. She'd bite your hand off."

"But didn't she give your brother her paw to hold?"

"That's different," I said. "Michael washed her and cleaned her wounds."

"And I suppose she sang her gratitude," Merle said and turned away from me.

We went back across Southern Boulevard. Merle saw the white skulls painted everywhere, on shoe repair shops, on the walls of tenements, on sidewalks, on the awnings of grocery stores. I still went around in my colors, but the Cannibals didn't bother me. I was a relic from the Stone Age.

Now we had our picnic on Indian Rock. We watched the rowers in the lake, their oars cutting into the water with a loud purr that left an echo. It was a poor people's paradise on a late Sunday afternoon in the middle of May. I opened the saddle bag. Merle insisted on sharing our feast with several neighbors on the massive rock. She'd brought extra paper cups. I leapt about the rock and filled everyone's cup with lemonade. I felt like the butler of Indian Rock as I pranced about with the thermos.

"Merle, my mother and father met here and fell in love on this rock."

"Then it will be our memento." And she called me darling for the first time.

I'm not sure why I shivered . . .

David picked her up at ten sharp in front of my stoop at Minford Place.

"Wait," Merle said. "Wolf boy, I haven't met your mother yet."

"Next time, Merle. Next time."

We hugged and kissed as I carried her into the car.

"Thank you, Jonah." David whispered in my ear.

I was puzzled. "For what?"

"I haven't seen her look so happy in a long time. She doesn't hate Connecticut. She just can't bear being away from you."

They drove off together. I went upstairs. Mom was in a sour mood.

"The pickle man proposed to me," Mom said. "I was tempted to run off with him and his fortune of barrels."

"Anita, you'd end up in the brine."

I could see the misery on her face, the same misery when Pop battled with her. "Are you ashamed of me, Jonah? Why haven't you introduced me to your girlfriend? You took her to meet your brother. Why not me?"

She was crying now. I held her in my arms. "I'm not ready, Anita. I was scared."

"Scared of what?" She had a bitterness in her voice.

"That you might not like her. And then I would be in a mess."

"Why would I not like a girl that you loved?"

EIGHTEEN

Anita

ANITA WAS A child prodigy. At the age of eleven, she began to attend Hunter College High School, the highest-rated public high school in the country. Hunter only accepted girls with the biggest brains, like my mom. Anita went to Hunter High from the seventh grade until she graduated. She lived on Bryant Avenue, with her two brothers and her father, who was a violin teacher. His name was Phillip, and he never left the apartment. His pupils came to him. He shuffled around in slippers. Mom had very little privacy. She slept on a board on the kitchen table. She had to cook and clean. Phillip barely earned a living with his violin lessons, so she started working at the chocolate factory on Saturdays and she's been there ever since.

Mom wavered between the sciences and the arts. She was a poet and a mathematical wizard. She still has a sheath of poems hidden away in her dresser. She never looks at them and has forbidden me to look. The poet in her has gone underground, I imagine, after years of neglect. But it wasn't always like that. When Mom was sixteen, she was a member of the honor society, as she prepared to enter Hunter College. She had offers of scholarships from all the fancy women's colleges, but she couldn't leave her father alone. He was absentminded and would misplace the bow of his fiddle, and it was Anita who always had to hunt for it, Anita who had to bathe her younger brothers and put them to bed. Her own mother had died of tuberculosis

a few months after Anita had entered Hunter High.

"My daughter will be another Einstein," Anita's mother—the grandma I never met—

had mumbled on her deathbed. She died at home. Phillip couldn't afford hospital care for her.

Anita had to scrape the money together to bury her own mother. Phillip refused a religious service. He was an atheist. But Anita sang the few Hebrew prayers she had memorized. She didn't want her mother buried without a prayer.

Anita longed to do research, to find a cure for tuberculosis and other diseases of the lungs and write poetry on the side. But it wasn't fated so. Soon she was seventeen. My mother was a prodigy. She was starting her sophomore year at Hunter College. And she went on a picnic with her girlfriends at Indian Rock. And there was Lorenzo without a shirt, sunbathing on that gigantic boulder. He was an auto mechanic who had his own garage. She'd never even gone out on a date. And here was a man with dark wavy hair and chiseled cheekbones. She looked at him once and all her future plans evaporated.

They went dancing at the Stardust Ballroom on Boston Road, above a movie palace, the RKO Chester. Lorenzo bought my mother an engagement ring. Phillip wouldn't let him into the apartment on Bryant Avenue. He called Lorenzo a wolf. That's what Mom remembered.

"He's a wolf, Anita. He'll swallow you and pick at your bones."

Phillip didn't attend the wedding. There was no wedding. Mom and Pop were married at Bronx Borough Hall, on the far side of Crotona Park, without a ceremony. They moved to Longfellow Avenue. Michael was born. Anita dropped out of Hunter College. She didn't like to talk about it.

"I'd rather have you and Michael than a Phi Beta Kappa Key and a career."

"But Anita, you have to work two shifts."

"I had to work two," she said. "Your father lost his garage."

I never met my two uncles. They sided with Phillip. And Anita had raised them. I only

saw my grandpa once. He was spying on us when we lived on Longfellow Avenue. He wore

slippers in the street. But he wouldn't come and say hello. There was no regret. I could see the rage in grandpa. Anita had violated him somehow.

And I had violated Mom. I should have introduced her to Merle on our first Sunday together. I was as stubborn as Grandpa Phillip. Sometimes I dream of his violin. He scrapes and scrapes with that lost bow of his.

I talked to David, told him how ashamed I was.

"Don't worry, kid."

He invited Mom to a Sunday brunch at Robbers Roost. I'd never been to a brunch before. David didn't include Alice and Flora. It was just the four of us. David, Merle, Mom, and me.

David ordered the best wine in the house. It had a pirate's name. Something like Lafite.

"Your son tells me you graduated from Hunter High. That's quite an achievement."

Mom blushed. She was always embarrassed by a compliment, as beautiful and brainy as she had once been—and still was. She was wearing a blue dress. Her hair was swept back so that we could all see the fine bones of her face, but years of drudgery had left a few scars. Her ankles had thickened and her fingers were sore from all that cherry-dipping at the chocolate factory.

"I was quite the little scholar, David. I had letters from half a dozen colleges asking me to apply."

"That's unique," David said. "It never happens."

"Oh, Hunter High had quite the reputation."

"It still does," David said. "Merle applied. And she got in. But she preferred Music and

Art. She said she didn't want to go to a school for girl geniuses."

Merle put her hand over her father's wrist. "Dad, stop boasting.... Anita, your son tells

me that you used to write poetry. Could you recite one for us? I'd love to hear it."

Mom was flustered now. "Merle, I couldn't remember a line. It's been so long since I stopped writing, all the words have fled."

Merle was persistent. "Couldn't you summon up a single line? It would give us so much pleasure."

A sadness erupted on Mom's face like a mysterious rash. "It's all gone blank, as if I had aphasia, and my mind was locked away in prison."

Mom had never used that word before. *Aphasia*. I listened hard and teased out what it meant. It was unbearable to lose the ability to read or understand words. Language suddenly became a scramble.

"My God," David said. "We all have bouts of aphasia. Sometimes, when I'm working late at night, I can't even recall the last sentence I wrote. But don't you think that the desire to write poetry will ever come back?"

"I doubt it, David. It's dead."

We had our salads in silence. Then Mom ordered roast duck in French and chatted with the owner of the restaurant.

"Mom," I said, "that's not aphasia. Where did you learn French?"

"At Hunter High."

She used her knife and fork like a princess, and I realized that Pop was the wild one, and

had made her wild. Mom could have eaten at Buckingham Palace.

David insisted on pouring the wine himself. Merle and I weren't allowed to drink at the Roost, but David gave each of us a sip from his glass.

"Anita," he said, "you must be worn to the bone working at a factory six days a week. Come work for me. I could use another copywriter."

Mom started to cry. It wasn't the way she cried when Michael was sent to Castle Billy. She was touched by David's gesture, more than touched. She wasn't used to kindness, having lived with a wild man like Pop, and with two wild sons and a father who declared himself an aristocrat in slippers. She wiped her eyes with David's handkerchief.

"I'd disappoint you, David."

"I doubt that," he said.

"It's Jonah who writes to the realtor and prepares the bills. I'm not even sure I could finish a sentence. The words escape me."

"I'm a gambler," he said. "I'll take that chance."

Merle was shrewd enough to see that her father was making Mom more and more upset. Mom had resigned herself to dipping cherries for the rest of her life. Her disappointment nourished her in some way I'll never understand. She loved Lorenzo. It didn't matter that he was at Creedmoor. He was her wild man, her wolf.

"Dad," Merle said, "why don't you hire me?"

"You're too bossy," David said. "I wouldn't be able to keep my own firm with you around."

DAVID INSISTED on driving us home to the Bronx. Merle sat in the front seat, and Mom and I sat in the back. I saw white skulls everywhere as soon as we entered our old terrain. David walked Mom upstairs while Merle and I remained in the car.

"Dad's a beast," Merle said. "He doesn't know a thing about your mother's life and offers her a job in the middle of our first meal. He behaved like a damn recruiter. I'll never forgive him."

"Ah," I said, "David was only trying to help. He could see how sore Mom's hands were."

"He pitied her, and she doesn't need pity. How could she possibly work in his office? She's a poet."

David returned to the car. I had never seen him so sad. "Jonah, we'll talk about this another time. It was like a first date, and I blew it... Merle, did you know that your father had such a big mouth?"

"Yes."

I leaned over, kissed her, and got out of the car.

David didn't want me to talk about Mom. I thanked him for my first brunch. He drove off with Merle and I went upstairs. Mom was in the kitchen.

"Jonah, are you ashamed of me?"

"No, Anita. Not at all."

"It's safer in the chocolate factory. I don't have to think. I couldn't write sentences about breakfast cereals. I'd rather die."

"Mom, David doesn't know you. As he said to me, it was like a first date."

I dreamt of Phillip again that night. He was dancing in his slippers. The strings of his violin had been ripped out. His bow scraped against a wooden box. It sounded like a cat scratching a screen. I woke with a slight fever. I went to M & A. Then I visited Wallenstein on Southern Boulevard. He was the Cannibals' tailor now; the Wolves didn't exist. But Wallenstein wasn't disloyal. Michael had given him whatever bounty he first had. We drank Earl Grey tea out of his tiny porcelain cups and had digestive biscuits.

"Wallenstein, I'm in a hole. I need some scratch."

His eyebrows perked. "Jonah boy, the Cannibals are my deliverers now."

"Make an exception," I said.

"Can't. They'll find out, son. They're cutthroats, they are."

So I had the Earl Grey and left. But I caught a surprise. Rosalind's funeral parlor had reopened. I raced to the Belevedere. The Widow was at her table with her shortcake and her Lipton's in the metal tea holder.

I sat down next to her without an invite. "Rosalind, I need a cash advance. Two hundred smackers."

She laughed in my face. I saw the gold fillings in her mouth. "I haven't rehired you, Jonah. What's the money for?"

"My mother, so she won't have to work two shifts at the chocolate factory."

Rosalind removed a thick envelope from her purse, and plucked out four fifty-dollar bills, each as crisp as the other.

"Say thank you, you handsome brat."

"It's a cash advance. When do I start?"

Her forehead ruffled. "Start what?"

"Drawing ghosts again."

"Soon," she said, with a forkful of shortcake in her mouth.

I WENT TO the chocolate factory. It should have had a sweet aroma. But you could catch the smell of sour milk chocolate a mile away. I saw women in white gloves and white masks, wearing blue smocks smeared with chocolate. They must have been on their coffee break. But I didn't see a coffee counter. I walked over to the manager. I knew Mom was in the middle of her second shift.

"I'd like to see Mrs. Salt. Please tell her that it's her son."

He saw my Silver Wolves blazer and he was gruff with me. "I can't take her off her station, kid. We'll be one dipper short. You'll have to sit until her next break."

So I remained in the outer room of what had been an abandoned shoe factory until it was converted to chocolates. It looked like an enormous grey shoebox right on the boulevard. The shoe factory had gone short during the Great Depression and sat there until Amazing Milk Chocolate grabbed up the shoebox at a city auction and started a manufacturing plant for glazed cherries dipped in a hot mold of milk chocolate from an enormous vat. The dipper had to work with precision and speed as the molds of chocolate moved along the assembly line machine like a choo-choo train.

I sat around for twenty minutes. The stink was unbearable. Mom left her station and walked into the outer room in her mask, gloves, and smock. She was wearing goggles to protect her from the tiny slivers that could scratch her eyeballs as the hardening molds of chocolate moved along the tracks of the assembly line.

She removed her goggles. "Jonah, what are you doing here?"

I waved the fifty-dollar bills. "Anita, you don't have to work a second shift anymore."

"Go home," she said and returned to her station.

I prepared a tuna salad with rye bread from the Russian bakery and slices of half-sour pickles from Jake's barrels. Mom opened the front door around midnight. Petulant, she wouldn't even say hello. She washed the chocolate gunk from her face in the bathroom sink, changed into her favorite robe, and only then did she enter the kitchen.

She began to eat the salad I had prepared. "I told you never to come to the factory. It's off limits."

"But I have news. You don't have to work a second shift. The Widow at the Belevedere gave me a cash advance."

"Einstein, if I don't work a second shift, I'll lose the first. That's the logic of Amazing Milk Chocolate."

"Then I'll rob a bank."

"Wonderful. Both my sons will be in prison. And I will run off with the pickle man."

Her face unfroze for the first time since she had sat down.

"But I'm grateful to your girlfriend and her father. That restaurant did something to me—Robbers Roost."

"Anita," I said, "I thought you had a miserable time."

"Not at all. David was delightful. And I adore Merle. I haven't been to a restaurant like that in years."

"He shouldn't have offered you a job," I said. "He doesn't even know you."

"He knows me well enough—through you. But it jolted me, his talk. It frightened me. And Jonah, the words are coming back. That lunch was like an electric shock. I could almost feel a poem in my head—at least a line or two."

I rose up from the table and nearly spilled the salad bowl. "Anita, then the aphasia is gone."

"Not completely."

"But it's a start," I said. And I took the peanut butter pie off the top of the fridge and cut a slice for Mom and myself.

She stared grimly at the pie. "Where did you get that?"

"From Gretel's."

It was the rival to the Russian bakery at the Jennings Street market. Mom never shopped there. She was loyal to the Russian bakers, as she was loyal to the pickle man.

She dug into the peanut butter pie with her fork, let the taste of it swirl in her mouth. "Jonah, it's delicious. We'll both be traitors, just this one time."

And the grimness of the hours imprisoned in that stinking shoebox on Southern boulevard fled from her face.

"Jonah darling," she said, "may I dare ask for a second slice?"

NINETEEN

At the Figaro

I'm not sure where the city's college students went to meet and do monkey business. But in the 1950s, when I was at M & A, the center of the world for high schoolers from all five boroughs was a single crossroad in Greenwich Village, Bleecker at MacDougal. There was a café at all four corners. I went to three, the Figaro, the San Remo, and the Borgia. The Borgia had the best food. But it was nowhere as popular as the Figaro, on the northwest corner. I wouldn't have gone there on my own. I would have kept to Crotona Park. But Merle was far more adventurous on our Sunday outings. Alice would pick me up at Minford Place, with Merle in the back seat, and drive us as close as she could get to the Café Figaro.

No matter how packed the Figaro was, the waiter always found a spot for Merle and me. There were also adults at the café, writers who sat there scribbling over a mug of coffee with a hat of hot foamy milk, sprinkled with cinnamon and specks of chocolate. It was called a cappuccino. And the Figaro claimed to have invented it. But it was a lie. Merle was an expert on cappuccinos. She first tasted coffee with a white cap of foam while on the terrace of a café during a trip to Milan with her mother and father. David and Alice were opera buffs, and they took Merle to La Scala, the opera house in Milan, to attend *Don Giovanni*, about a notorious seducer of women who ends up burnt to a crisp in hell. We had seducers like that in the Bronx, maybe not on Don Giovanni's scale. None of them, as far as I know, were sent to hell. But they were all beaten by the husbands, uncles, and brothers of the women they had seduced. It wasn't a pretty sight. The Don Giovanni I recalled had a limp for the rest of his life . . .

We shared a slice of the Figaro's cheesecake. I liked it. But I preferred Gretel's peanut butter pie. Phyllis Pearl was at a table near the bar, conspiring with the prominent editors of other high school papers. The Figaro must have been a hot spot for editors-in-chief. But I was wrong. The other girls with Phyllis were part of a rebel group at Parkchester, the housing development in the Bronx that excluded Black families. And Phyllis was preparing a petition that would end Parkchester's exclusion clause.

She hadn't seen Merle in months. It took her five minutes to get to our table. That's how little space there was at the Figaro after school hours. We signed Phyllis' petition, but we weren't residents of Parkchester.

"Signatures," Phyllis said, "signatures always help." She tasted Merle's cappuccino and licked her lips. "What is that?"

"Coffee steamed with milk. The Figaro stole the formula. Soon they'll swear they invented ice cream."

But our editor-in-chief was always prepared. "You aren't a vagabond, Merle. Where did you go when you left M & A?"

"Brewster Academy," Merle said.

"It has an excellent reputation," Phyllis said.

"Yes, we're volleyball champs."

Phyllis persisted. "Couldn't you write an article about your stay at Brewster for *Overtone*? You're still one of us in spirit. It would fascinate our readers."

"I'll think about it," Merle said, as she watched Phyllis maneuver like a rat in a maze until she got back to her table of rebels. "Phyllis has some nerve."

"But she isn't wrong. Readers would be fascinated."

Merle blinked her eyes like Ophelia. "My God. I almost forgot. You're a member of *Overtone*, too."

Other Music and Arters appeared, paying court to a former classmate.

It was strange, having one corner of the city overrun with high schoolers. The Figaro didn't feel like a hangout or a haven; it seemed as if we held the lease. The Figaro catered to us and a couple of scribblers who sat far from the window.

"Merle, do you realize that we're the landlords of this crossroad? We own Bleecker *and* MacDougal."

"Not the landlords, Jonah. Just the chief clients. The Figaro and the Borgia would collapse without the high school brigade."

We had our second cappuccino and left. The streets were packed with high schoolers all the way to Washington Square Park. It was like a fashion show. Some were dressed as clowns, others came as acrobats with their own high wires. One girl from the High School of Fashion came as Marie Antoinette, wearing a wig and a long dress encrusted with phony jewels. She had a whole league of followers, who danced around her and bowed to her every whim. I wasn't a fool. Marie Antoinette was the queen who brought down the French monarchy. She told the starving people from the countryside to eat cake if they couldn't find bread. But Gretel's peanut butter pie didn't exist in the eighteenth century. And the monarchy fell.

The park was loaded with street venders. They had every sort of merchandise for sale. Bags of marijuana, slide projectors with pornographic scenes, rock candy, roasted marshmallows, cowboy boots and neckerchiefs, and marionettes. The marionettes appealed to me. They didn't look manufactured. They were carved by a craftsman and could be moved by strings connected to their hands and feet. I couldn't find the standard marionettes—Pinocchio or Cinderella. These dolls were contemporary. I recognized Joker. I recognized Jay Gatsby in his white linen suit. I recognized Lois Lane. Most of all, I recognized the marionettist. It was Merriman, wearing a cowboy neckerchief. He didn't sneak around with his marionettes and hide himself from us.

"Mr. M," Merle asked, "what the hell are you doing here?"

"Making ends meet."

He pulled Joker's strings and had the marionette sit in Merle's lap.

She pressed him. "But you have a salary."

"And a wife who wants custody of the kids. Besides, I love to carve the puppets and bind then to their strings."

She pressed him further. "And you do puppet shows in the park?"

"No, Merle, I'm not an entertainer. I sell the marionettes."

"Then I'll buy one," Merle said. "Name your price, Mr. M."

I could see how unsettled Merriman was. It baffled me at first. Merle and I admired him so much, and here he was in the park, another merchant with his wooden dolls, probably making sales pitches. I couldn't imagine the author of *Jonathan's Journey* as a pitchman, a hawker in the streets.

Merle continued to press him. "Haven't other Music and Arters recognized you?"

"Not yet. They aren't as clever as Jonah and you. They haven't seen beyond my disguise."

"But you aren't wearing a disguise."

"Yes I am," he said. "Jonah, why are you so silent?"

I was stupefied. "I never thought of you having a family and family troubles. I imagined you living in a garret, correcting our papers and working on your second novel."

"But I do live in a garret—now. Diane has left me penniless. I have to pay for her lawyers and can't afford one of my own. At first I carved the marionettes for Davy—my little one—and his sister, Delia, but they weren't entertained at all. They're both on Diane's side."

"Mr. M," I asked, "did you commit a crime?"

"Yes. I fell out of love with my wife. I had more affection for my students than for her."

"That is a crime," Merle said. "We can't provide you with a home. And you've lost the one you had. I can't bear to look at you as a street merchant. Come with me."

Merriman was lost in a dream. He hadn't expected us to find him as a vender at Washington Square Park. "What about my dolls?"

"Oh, my Dad will buy the whole lot. They'll make perfect Christmas presents."

Merriman folded his marionettes, wrapped their strings around them, and put them into a suitcase that reminded me of a coffin at Rosalind's funeral parlor. But this coffin had wheels.

We returned to the Figaro. It was much less crowded. The mass exodus of high schoolers was over for this afternoon. They must have gone to another location or back to the outer boroughs. I couldn't understand the appeal of Bleecker at MacDougal. It was as if the entire high school population was a swarm of bees that had to touch and then disconnect. The touching was essential.

Merle scolded Mr. Merriman. She was brutal with him. She could afford to be now that

she wasn't in his class. "You have two young children."

"They hate me," he said.

"Children don't hate without a reason. You abandoned them. Mr. M, go back to your wife."

"She doesn't want me."

"Woo her again."

He laughed. "You ought to join Jonah's gang. You'd make an excellent commandant."

"Sir," I said, "I don't have a gang. The Wolves have been wiped out. The Cannibals painted white skulls all over the place."

"That's a pity," Merriman said, with cappucchino foam on his mouth.

DAVID DID BUY up Merriman's entire stock of marionettes. But he didn't give them out to his clients as Christmas presents. He installed them around the apartment at the Majestic. Joker sat on a windowsill. Jay Gatsby was on the dining room table, as a reminder of what would happen to David if he failed. Lois Lane hung from the door that led to the kitchen. Merle didn't want any of the dolls for herself. She just wanted them to be there when she got back from Brewster on Saturday nights.

Merriman did make amends with his wife. He must have followed Merle's advice and wooed Diane with the same passion he had in class. His children adored him now. The divorce lawyers were shoved out of the way. He got rid of his garret on Washington Square. Diane fixed up his old office in their five-room flat on Riverside Drive. He had a view of the Hudson, and he looked out at the wind creating foam on the water like the "caps" on our coffee cups at the Figaro, as he worked on a novel he would never complete. His story had been told and couldn't be told again. He would walk to M & A from his apartment with a briefcase stuffed with student compositions he had corrected in red ink.

I was never sure whether Merle and I had liberated Mr. Merriman or created a quiet monster. The marionettes must have been a reminder of his earlier life on the farm. David Messenger asked for more. He told me that he had talked to the marionettes, that they were like living creatures. He never pulled the strings. He would let them sit there.

But Merriman had stopped carving these dolls. He invited our entire gang—Merle, David, Alice, myself, and my mom—to Riverside Drive for a Sunday brunch. The children, Davy and Delia, were at our feet. I felt that I had suddenly acquired a new family. David had become Tom Merriman's patron. But Mr. M had no intention of carving new marionettes, no matter what David offered him.

It was Merriman himself who had come downstairs to greet our gang. The lobby was very ornate. I traced all the blue veins in the marble.

Mom and Diane Merriman gazed at one another as soon as David opened the door. They both had a puzzled look. And then they smiled with absolute joy.

"Diane Hiller," Mom said.

"I'm Merriman now," Diane said.

They both had been classmates at Hunter High and best friends. They were inseparable until Diane went off to Vassar College in Poughkeepsie and Mom met Lorenzo on Indian Rock.

They abandoned us for ten minutes, left us standing near the door, strolled around the apartment with their arms around each other, and then returned.

"Anita, I kept looking for your poems to appear. I would open *The New Yorker* every

week, expecting to find a poem by my Anita. I knew you had married a heartthrob. Lorenzo, isn't it? Why isn't he here now?"

"My husband had a breakdown. He's at Creedmoor."

"I'm so sorry," Diane said. "But will you read us some of your poems when we have bagels and lox?"

Merriman frowned. "Honey, Mrs. Salt hasn't come here to entertain us."

"That's idiotic," Diane said. "Anita loves to read her poems. She was the class poet, for God's sake. The poet laureate of Hunter High."

I could feel the tension build. "Diane," Mom said, in a voice that was hardly a whisper, "I stopped writing years ago."

"That's no problem," Diane said. "There are plenty of poems in our yearbook. I can recite then for you."

"I'd rather you didn't, Diane," Mom said. "They're juvenilia. I wouldn't want them read aloud."

The tension died after that. Mom seemed pleased about the accidental reunion with an old high school chum.

The adults drank champagne. Merle and I were allowed two sips. Otherwise we had grape juice and a twist of lemon with the two kids. Merriman sat in an armchair. He reminded me of Lorenzo for a moment with his blank stare. David did most of the talking. He wanted to buy more of Merriman's marionettes.

"You know, I could get you a gallery, Tom. Art like yours has come into fashion."

"I'll think about it, David." But he had no intention of carving more marionettes. Mostly

he wanted to talk to Merle. Colleges didn't have wheelchair ramps.

"Oh, Dad's ingenious," Merle said. "He'll have the colleges come to me. He'll send a chauffeur to kidnap the professors. I'll get my degree."

But I could feel a silence begin to surround Tom Merriman, as if a piece of him was back at that hardscrabble farm in Nebraska, a piece of him had never left. He'd been sent off to the University of Chicago as a pioneer, a boy from the plains. And the sound of the plains, the bitter winds, must still have been in his blood. He was such a good teacher because he gave so much of himself to his students; the rest of him was prairie dust.

We had bagels and lox and Russian coffee cake from Zabar's, a refined version of the Jennings Street market. Zabar's didn't have Jake the pickle man. It didn't have live cod swimming in fish tanks. It didn't have mountains of sawdust. It had Manhattan's veneer.

We stayed five hours.

It was Merriman who carried Merle across the lobby and into David's Cadillac.

"See what happens when you scold somebody? I'm a family man again."

"Stay that way."

"I will," he said, as he slid Merle into the back seat. The Nebraska farm boy would always be in him. No wonder *Jonathan's Journey* had sunk. Merriman had his own journey to complete.

TWENTY

King of the Crag

I DIDN'T NOTICE it at first. Mom had bought a notebook at Woolworth's. She took it with her to the chocolate factory. She wasn't like the writers at the Figaro or the Belevedere. She didn't drink Lipton's or sit with a cappuccino as she scratched words on paper. Anita wrote on the sly, during her lunch and coffee breaks at the factory, or she would sing the words to herself while she was dipping cherries at her station.

The aphasia was gone.

I showed Mom all my compositions, all the check marks I got from Merriman, all the bylines I had shared with Merle in *Overtone*. She didn't make any corrections or comment on my sentences or Merle's, before Merle left our Castle for Connecticut.

"Jonah, you have the gift. Nourish it."

I'm not sure why I was cross with her. "You haven't nourished yours." Maybe I was jealous of my own mother, and the talent I must have sensed in her, the talent that lay underground so long. But she didn't return home that night with a sad crease on her brow. We ate whatever was in the fridge.

"Anita, why can't you show me what you're writing?"

"I'm not ready. I have to relearn whatever I lost. I'm a bird with broken wings. I can't soar. And I want to soar."

Pop had nearly defeated her. Her love for him had consumed my mom. Both of us were beginning to recover from his abuse. And then Pop reappeared. He'd been given the green light, otherwise known as the Thorazine cure. Psych hospitals were emptying their back wards. They'd found their miracle drug. Pop was dumped onto Minford Place from an ambulance. He returned to his chair. Creedmoor must have misplaced his bundle of clothes. He was wearing hospital pajamas with a string around his belly. His hair hadn't been cut. He looked like a warrior with missing teeth. I made Pop a salad with Jake's half-sour pickles.

I didn't expect any thanks. "You," he said, "where's my boy?"

"In Castle Billy, Pop. You know that."

Pop didn't want me to put on any lights. He sat in the dark. I figured the Thorazine had made him a zombie. But he let out a soft cry when he heard Mom's footsteps in the hall. Mom saw him there in the shadows. She jumped right into his lap. I thought Pop's knees would break. He wasn't a zombie at all.

"Jonah," she said, "put on some lights. We aren't living in a morgue."

I was embarrassed to see Mom and Pop kiss. They were like kids on a couch at our old headquarters.

"Sourpuss," Mom said, mussing Pop's hair, "I missed you so much."

All that brittle coldness I had seen at Creedmoor disappeared in a second.

"Hey, Jonah," Mom said, "why are you letting Lorenzo sit in lousy stinking pajamas? Did you forget you had a father?"

She undressed him with her own sore hands and walked him to the bathtub. She sat him down, ran the water, shampooed his hair, and scrubbed him with a bath brush. Each of her movements was an act of love. She wasn't thinking about poetry, about the violent music that the different scramble of words could make. She was thinking about Pop. He didn't sleep in his armchair that night.

We had breakfast together on Sunday morning. Pop had his scrambled eggs with ketchup. We found his homburg in the closet. We found the double-breasted suit he liked to wear at the Brooklyn Navy Yard during the war. He was Lorenzo Salt again, the ladykiller. Mom searched everywhere and found his dressy shoes in the broom closet. She sat cross-legged on the living room rug and shined his shoes with a rag and a can of polish. She kidnapped my Old Man, dragged me along, and we went on a promenade together around Indian Lake.

Anita was bold. The dentistry at Creedmoor must have been terrible, because Pop had a mouth full of chipped or missing teeth. But that didn't cut into the swagger he had in his Florsheim shoes. Even after a ton of Thorazine and his time in the back wards, Pop was the best-looking stud in Crotona Park.

"Anita, remember when you flirted with me?"

"I did not flirt," Mom said. It was a game the two of them liked to play.

"I was minding my own business on Indian Rock."

"Sure," she said. "You had your eye on me, Lorenzo Salt."

"Impossible," Pop said. "I was innocent as a lamb."

"Yeah," Mom said. "Some lamb."

The wives on the benches stared at Lorenzo in his double-breasted suit. He didn't stare back. Mom was happier than I'd seen her in a long time. She had all the poetry she wanted—in Lorenzo's looks.

IT COULDN'T last. Maybe Pop needed a doctor from Creedmoor to adjust his dose of Thorazine. He grew more and more morose in his armchair. He attacked Mom after he'd been home a week, accused her of going out on dates with the manager of Amazing Milk Chocolate. I'd seen the manager. He didn't have Pop's appeal. But the Thorazine, whatever dose, had turned Pop's brain to mud, mud with violence mixed in. He chased Mom around with a kitchen knife. It wasn't a joke. I grabbed a towel, warded off his thrusts. I couldn't whack my own father. But he nearly chopped my arm off.

"You little bastard," he said. "You're not my son. Anita had you while I was at the Navy Yard." He must have been in a Thorazine daze. I was four years old when he worked at the Yard. I slapped the knife out of his hand with one swipe of the towel. Then I called the Cap.

He arrived in twenty minutes. "Mrs. Salt," he said, "you'll have to sign a complaint."

"I can't," Mom said. "I can't do it."

Captain Shelly pleaded with her. "Jonah's a juvie. He wouldn't have much punch in court."

But the Cap could see how sad and broken Mom was. Lorenzo's sudden return from Creedmoor was like a magical event. Mom dreamed of having a husband again. And here he was back to brooding in his chair, with dark fantasies in his brain, disaster in his heart.

"Okay," the Cap said, "I'll handle the paperwork."

He took Pop away. I was confused as ever. I couldn't tell if the Cap was my worst enemy or my best friend. Maybe he was both.

I couldn't cheer Mom up. She took out her notebook, sat at her tiny writing desk, and started to scribble. The scratch of her pen must have kept her from going out of her mind. She found Lorenzo on a rock, and lost him again and again and again. She sang the words this time,
like a witch—a kind witch—at work:

> *The flash of sun razor sharp.*
> *Boulders big as mountain crags,*
> *A sun god with curly hair.*

She fell asleep at her writing desk. She must have been worn to the bone, working all those hours, trying to take care of Lorenzo, restoring their romance. The excitement of it, and then that letdown, as Pop's jealous rages returned, had exhausted her. I carried her into the bedroom, put the covers over her, and set the alarm clock. I didn't feel much like sleeping. I loved seeing Pop in his double-breasted suit, handsome as a movie star, even without his teeth. And then that explosion. I think it began to build the moment he saw me. I was the interloper in the house, the evil son. Maybe Pop was right.

I sat beside Mom's bed and woke her at a quarter to six. I didn't really need an alarm clock. I washed her face with a hand towel, removed the crust from her eyes. It took her a while to recognize me. That's how groggy she was. I didn't want to imagine what her dreams must have been like.

"Jonah, where am I?"

"On Minford Place, Mom, where you belong."

Her eyes opened wide without all the crust. "Did I sleep in my clothes?"

"Yeah, Anita, I put you to bed."

She looked around her, like a stranger might have done. "Where's Lorenzo?"

"Back at Creedmoor. Mom, he chased you around the kitchen—with a knife."

"And you called the savior, Captain Shelly. It was Shelly who got Michael to enlist,

Shelly who whispered in his ear. Michael hadn't done anything wrong."

I didn't tell Mom how Michael went into business with Wallenstein, the tailor, how he ripped off rear view mirrors from parked cars and brought them to Wallenstein, the biggest fence in the Bronx. The tailor was immune. The mirrors couldn't have been traced to him. He sat behind a maze of lawyers and cops. And Michael didn't steal to replenish Mom or himself. He used the money from Wallenstein to help feed old ladies and retired old men on the top floor apartments who would have starved without Michael's help. He was our Robin Hood. We had Crotona Park. But we didn't have Sherwood Forest, where an outlaw-general could hide.

I had raisin bran with Mom. She didn't have time to shower or change her clothes. But she wouldn't forget her notebook from Woolworth's. I was glad she'd gone back to writing. Her poems were like a picture show. She could recapture the moment she met Lorenzo on Indian Rock, recapture it with her own gift of words. It was a gift. Each word had a sound, a texture, its own image on the page. I wasn't a poet. I was a storyteller. I could relive Mom's romance in a million ways. But I couldn't have found the words to describe the dazzle of the sun on Lorenzo's face the moment she first saw him. Only Mom could do that.

I collected my books and went to the Castle. M & A wasn't much fun without Merle. I worked on *Overtone*, helped the cubbies write their articles about events that concerned high schoolers, scraping off each word that was unnecessary. There was even an article about "the Carnival," as the four corners of Bleecker at MacDougal were called.

I wrote that article myself, without a byline. I wanted to be anonymous, an observer with my own private ability to reflect. I noticed that it was the students with the best grades, those who worked the hardest, who went to the Figaro and the Borgia, and paraded around Bleecker in outrageous costumes. There was a word I discovered in the dictionary. *Bacchanal*. It meant a moment of wild, wild revelry. It didn't matter to me where the word came from. It only mattered that the Carnival inside and outside the corner cafés on Bleecker was a bacchanal. It was the academic pressure on those students destined for the most prestigious colleges in the country that created the Bleecker Street Bacchanal.

The constant studying, the exams, the fear of failure, among other things, left us half-crazed. So we needed our corner of Manhattan, where we had control over the terrain, where we could sit, drink white-capped coffee. act snotty to waiters and busboys at the Figaro, or prance around dressed as Marie Antoinette or a soldier of fortune, or any other figure rooted in our imagination.

There was no nostalgia about the Bacchanal. Once students had their SAT scores and got an acceptance slip from a college of their choice, they rarely returned to the Figaro, or had any role in the Carnival. "It was for the strivers," I wrote, "for those who were still uncertain of their future. The Figaro eased that uncertainty, and the Carnival gave them a sense of belonging somewhere, of doing whatever they wanted on their own turf."

It made us members of one stupendous street gang. But I didn't write this in my article. It would have shocked Dean Amanda and the Parents Association. After that issue of *Overtone* was put to bed, the dean called me into her office without Phyllis Pearl.

"Jonah," she said, "your article was a revelation. I'd heard of the Figaro, of course, but I did not know that such a massive carnival of high school students existed in Manhattan. Your insights were sensational."

They were the insights of a gang member who had watched his gang disappear. I couldn't have written that article without the Cannibals and the Silver Wolves.

"You know that Phyllis' term as editor-in-chief will expire at the end of June. And I will pick *Overtone*'s new editor."

I was confused. "I thought that was Mr. Merriman's job."

"Ah, but I have final say."

And now I was really rattled. Amanda knew that my rise to *Overtone*'s editor-in-chief would be a tremendous plus on my college applications, more important than my SATs. But I would have had to manage the newspaper without Merle. And I couldn't even rely on Phyllis as an agitator.

I had Mom and Merle to consider. I might not have my Sundays clear if I was picked as editor-in-chief. I was second in command of a gang that didn't exist. White skulls were painted everywhere I walked in the Bronx. They were on the turnstiles at the 174th Street El, they were on the stoop of our building. I had to get the chalk faces off our turf before I could even consider Amanda's proposal.

TWENTY-ONE

Cannibals

It could have been laziness or cruelty or the mindless swagger of being lords of a new domain, but the Cannibals didn't behave like chieftains. More like swindlers and thieves. Maybe they were blind to their own insolence. Percival had come out of retirement and gone back to boxing in Crotona Park. His knuckles had healed. They had little bumps on them, like horns, and he would hone them with sandpaper. He worried that his knuckles would betray him during his first match after that sit in the infirmary at Spofford. His opponent, the bare-knuckle champion of Minneapolis, had never lost a fight. He was six inches taller than Percival and his knuckles were like enormous acorns. Kid Galahad, as he was known, was the heavy favorite. The odds were six to one. I bet what little I had on Percival.

The park was packed. Every hill was swollen with people. Strangers had come on long bus rides to see what Percival had left. I watched the match with them. It should have been a slaughter. Galahad landed with both fists. Percival staggered, and I could hear the cries of dismay from every corner of the park, but Percival didn't fall. He absorbed the blows and hit back. Galahad's own punches had tired him. He could barely raise his fists. He began to spin around in that fighters' circle of sand. His trainers had to stop the match.

I couldn't get near Percival for another twenty minutes. The Cannibals wanted to parade him around the park. But he was wise enough to resist. He sat on Indian Rock with ice packs on both cheeks. Finally I got to him.

"Congratulations, Percy."

One of his eyes was completely shut. He still managed to smile. "I hope you bet on me, kid."

"Six to one," I said. "But there's another matter. Percy, the Cannibals have been running wild. They steal candy bars from corner groceries, make off with tubs of butter. They seized the boathouse in the park, and now no one can rent a rowboat. They won't pay for their coffee and pie at the Belevedere. They've turned the El station into their private toll bridge. Can't you do something?"

He shrugged his shoulders. There were spots of blood on the victory robe he wore.

"What can I do, kid? It's the spoils of war."

THE CHALK FACES didn't bother Mom as she went to work. She must have been on Percival's untouchable list. Or maybe it was random. I didn't want Merle to come into the neighborhood on our Sunday outings. But she insisted. "I'm sick of Central Park West. All you see are poodles pissing in the street."

So Alice brought her in the Cadillac. But ten minutes after she showed up, a band of chalk faces shoved me aside and raced off with Merle and her chariot, creating havoc as they ran across Boston Road. They abandoned her near a mailbox, the chariot tipped to one side, with Merle half in and half out of her seat. I didn't have any tools. But I managed to fix one of the wheels and help her back into the chair.

She could tell how upset I was.

"Jonah, it was just a prank."

"Weren't you scared?"

She turned away from me. "A little."

We went back to Minford Place.

"I don't want to hide upstairs," she said.

We visited the Jennings Street market. The Cannibals had left their markers—the painted skulls—but none of their members were around. I introduced her to Jake. The pickle man was very busy, but he kept one eye on Merle as he filled customers' jars with pickles and brine.

"Mr. Salt, it's unjust to entice a pickle man with such a beautiful maiden when I have so much work to do."

"Jake, Merle is not a maiden, and since when am I Mr. Salt?"

"It's a name," he said, "just a name." He handed Merle a half-sour pickle dipped in brine, and a napkin to go with it.

Merle hadn't really recovered from that escapade with the Cannibals. I could see the terror in her eyes. I dragged her into the Russian bakery, and sat with her at its one and only table. We had to serve ourselves. I grabbed spoons and forks and saucers from the counter. We had coffee and marble cake, with its black and white "brick" made from vanilla and chocolate batter. Her hand shook as she fed herself a slice of marble cake.

Then we returned to Central Park West in a cab. The Cannibals had ruined our Sunday together. I didn't stay for dinner at the Messengers. I had to think. I sat on the train and realized that I couldn't go to Michael or Captain Shelly. Neither could help me now.

WENT TO Amanda. I wasn't wishy-washy. I told her that I couldn't wait to be editor-in-chief of *Overtone*. Phyllis resigned. She wanted to end her rule of red pencils. I ended it for her. Martin Fitzgerald, the current police commissioner, had accepted to give the graduation speech at Music and Art. "Fitz," as he was known, had political ambitions. I learned that from Phyllis. He wanted to run for mayor. That's why he accepted so many speaking engagements.

I never told Amanda that I intended to interview him for *Overtone*. I did tell Merriman. I wouldn't lie to him.

"I don't give a damn what Fitz might do for the city as mayor. I want him to get the Cannibals as far from Minford Place as he can."

"Careful," Merriman said. "He might feel that you're trying to interfere."

"I am interfering."

"Then why would he see you?"

"Because," I said, "I'm *Overtone*'s editor-in-chief."

I called police headquarters at 240 Centre Street. I was able to get Fitz's assistant secretary on the line. She told me how busy the Commissioner was until I gave her my title—editor-in-chief. She had no idea what *Overtone* was. But it seemed to intimidate her.

"Mr. Salt, I think the Commissioner can squeeze you in for five minutes."

She put me down on Fitz's calendar.

I had to be a silver wolf, so I wore moccasins and one of Michael's suits. I took the subway to Franklin Street and walked to police headquarters. I passed between the two stone lions, gave my name at the door, went up one side of a twin marble staircase—police headquarters looked like a palace with its lanterns, its chandelier, and a rotunda that reached the roof. It had a dome with sunlight that seemed to pierce the walls. It had portraits of earlier Police Commissioners. I recognized Teddy Roosevelt's mustache within one of the gold frames. I never realized that the Rough Rider who became President had also been a Police Commissioner.

I was met by a clerk at the top of the stairs, and sat on a bench outside the Commissioner's office. I must have waited half an hour. Then another clerk, with a police badge, escorted me in.

Fitz was huge. He came out from behind his desk to greet me. He had big grey eyes, big hands, big feet, and each nostril was as huge as the bowl of a tobacco pipe. I wondered if he could have beaten Percival in a bare-knuckle bout. A handsome man with red hair, I doubt he was much older than forty. He must have sniffed "a meteoric political future for himself," as Mr. Merriman once remarked about Teddy Roosevelt.

I liked Fitz's smile.

"You're a little young to be a police reporter," he said.

"But I'm not a police reporter, Commissioner Fitzgerald. I'm editor of a student newspaper. *Overtone*."

His eyebrows leapt. "Then why would you want to interview a Police Commissioner? And you can call me Fitz. Everybody else does."

"You're scheduled to speak at my high school. Music and Art."

His eyebrows leapt again. "Never heard of it." He shouted for his secretary. "Clara, come in here."

A woman with short hair rushed into the office.

"Clara, did you book me to speak at a place called Music and Art?"

His secretary hesitated for a moment. "I did, sir. You insisted."

The Commissioner scratched his head. "That's odd. I can't remember a thing. Music and Art..."

His secretary left with a pained look. But Fitz was completely jovial.

He peeked at his appointment book. "Well, my young friend, what would you like to know? We fight crime. That is our mission. I can show you our latest reports. Burglaries are up, and homicides are way down. Did you know that the overwhelming majority of homicides are domestic?"

"You mean family fights, Fitz?"

"That's exactly what I mean. We can only do something when we're called in. And most of the time it's too late."

"Well, there's a domestic quarrel in my neighborhood, Fitz."

He grew cautious. "How so?"

"The Webster Avenue Cannibals are trying to claim the South Bronx. And so far they're succeeding."

All his joviality was gone. "Who are these Cannibals?"

"A street gang, Fitz. The biggest in the Bronx."

His eyes narrowed as he stared at me. "That doesn't come to my table, son. It's strictly local. A precinct matter."

But I had the big blustering Police Commissioner in my palm. It bothered me that he would speak at a school he had never heard about.

"It's not local to us, Fitz. It's life and death."

He tried to steer the conversation away from the Cannibals. He pounded on the blotter of his big oak desk with his enormous fist and said, "Do you realize, son, that I'm sitting where Teddy Roosevelt sat? This was his desk. I took it out of storage. It was gathering dust in a warehouse. He chased after criminals on the back of a fire truck. Best damn commissioner we ever had. He had fistfights with corrupt cops. No one napped on the job with Commissioner Ted around. I've been battling corruption myself. I remember now. Music and Art. My grandmother graduated from there."

I watched the anger in him build. I had to be cautious. "I doubt that, sir. The school didn't open until 1936. But there might have been a high school just like it where your grandma went."

"That's it!" he said. "An earlier twin."

He shouted for his secretary again. "Clara, will you come in and show the young reporter out?"

Clara arrived in a huff. She escorted me to the edge of the double staircase. "You'll have to forgive him," she said. "It's an impossible job. The city's five boroughs are like five different kingdoms, with different needs. He sits behind that desk and broods."

I had a different take. Fitz was isolated in his palace,

isolated and alone. Each captain presided over his precinct, had his own private roost. Fitz should have known about the Cannibals, and he knew nothing at all. He had the polished handles of Teddy Roosevelt's desk to console him.

THEY EVEN BOTHERED the pickle man now. The chalk faces surrounded him, reached into his purse, and plucked as many dollars as they wanted. They stole entire cartons of charlotte russes from the Russian bakery. The cops did eventually arrive. They scribbled in their notebooks, but no arrests were ever made.

I set my alarm and walked Mom to work. I stopped at the Belevedere after school or went down to the Figaro. I'd become addicted to coffee with a snowcap on top. But it wasn't much fun without Merle. I wore my Silver Wolves jacket, which was as much of an antique as Teddy Roosevelt's desk. It had the two yellow eyes that Wallenstein had stitched onto the back. That was my costume for the Carnival.

I was a veteran now. I knit together my interview with Fitz. I wrote about the twin stone lions, the twin marble staircase, my sense of police headquarters as a lavish nineteenth century palace. I even wrote how Fitz was the guardian of all five boroughs, how he wandered through the toughest neighborhoods. I turned him into another Teddy Roosevelt. I attached a photo of Fitz that one of my cubs got from the police archives, Fitz behind Teddy Roosevelt's desk. I gave him the entire front page of *Overtone*:
TOP COP TO VISIT CASTLE ON THE HILL.

Dean Amanda was delighted. "Ah, the details, Jonah,

the details are divine." She said that my interview with Fitz would enchant all our readers. But Mr. Merriman knew how fraudulent it was.

"He's a son of a bitch, isn't he?"

"Fitz wants to be mayor. He doesn't give a damn about Music and Art."

"Phyllis would have flayed him alive," Merriman said.

"Maybe not. It's *Overtone*."

I returned to the barracks our neighborhood had become.

TWENTY-TWO

Yellow Eyes

Fitz arrived at graduation surrounded by his deputies. They all wore white gloves. He stood on the podium with all his power as Police Commissioner. He dreamt of a time when every officer in the NYPD would be a college graduate. "Brains, that's what we need. We can teach the rough stuff. But I want officers with imagination and mercy in their hearts." Parents and graduates clapped and cheered. I stood in the back of the auditorium with my cubs. Merriman was beside us.

"What a bullshit artist," Merriman whispered. "Can you imagine a bunch of Yalies patrolling the city streets? And mercy doesn't come with a college degree."

"He's a politician," I said. "A pitchman."

"Bullshit artist is better."

I watched the graduates in their mortarboards and rented gowns of burgundy and light blue. I doubt they would have considered entering the Police Academy after four years of college. And I had to wonder why Michael didn't get into Music and Art. His sketches couldn't have been any worse than mine. And Michael was the big brain of Hermann Ridder Junior High, even while he was lord of the Silver Wolves, though his grades did suffer.

Maybe Fitz wasn't so wrong. Cops with college degrees.

I treated my cubs to egg creams at the soda shop down the hill from Convent Avenue. I was glad I didn't have to look at white skulls painted on every other wall. I was back to sketching ghosts for the Widow at her funeral parlor, so I had plenty of pocket money, even after I gave Mom half of what I earned to help pay for groceries and the rent. And I also had enough to raid the canteen at Castle Billy for Michael and get him his favorite caramels.

But I couldn't ask Alice Messenger to drive Merle to the South Bronx and have another Sunday ruined by the Cannibals. So David took control. He drove us to the Catskill Mountains, where he'd gone with his family as a little boy. His family had rented a bungalow every summer near Monticello, New York, and "borrowed" a swimming hole at dinner time. The swimming hole belonged to a Catskills summer resort, the Maple Grove, and David would swim in that hole—a pond—while the Maple Grove's guests were at dinner. He remembered crossing a cow pasture and wiggling through a wire fence with his brothers and walking on a dirt road to get to the hole. He could hear the chatter coming from the hotel dining room. But no one ever interfered with David while he was at the swimming hole. He and his brothers would capture frogs and toss them back into the water. He could still recall the flight of the frogs, how their legs spun in the air. It was the highlight of his summer, trespassing on Maple Grove property, and swimming in the pond, with the echo of dishes clattering in his ears.

The summer resort sat empty now, but the pond hadn't disappeared. So David drove a little past Monticello, then followed a dirt road as far as we could get. And we walked the rest of the way, with Merle in the wheelchair. Flora had packed a picnic basket, while Alice carried a thermos of lemonade and several blankets. David and I wore our trunks under our shirts and pants, while the women came to the Catskills in bathrobes and slippers, with their bathing suits under the robes.

I could hear the frogs croak the nearer we got to the pond. It was, as David said, a hole. It had no particular shape. Merle swam swiftly, and I, a city boy, had clumsy strokes. I splashed around, frightening the frogs, while Merle moved in an unwavering line. It was like watching a mermaid.

SOME PEOPLE say that Fitz rode along Boston Road with a fleet of sedans, that the fleet stopped outside Hermann Ridder, that Fitz got out of his sedan and ran his finger along the white skull painted on one of Ridder's walls, that he cursed, got back into his sedan, and rode away. It sounds like a myth to me. I wouldn't be surprised if Fitz never saw the South Bronx, that he couldn't have told you where Minford Place or the Jennings Street market was, that he'd never had a pickle from the pickle man. I suspect that a deputy chief inspector got wind of what the Cannibals were doing, and it went down the chain of command.
I can't think of another explanation. There was no sudden jolt, no shift in the landscape. The ravage of white skulls remained. But there were less and less Cannibals on our

streets. The gang vacated our clubhouse and left their girlfriends behind. An army of street cleaners from the city's Sanitation Department appeared one day and began scraping off the white skulls. It took two weeks of solid work. Cannibals still sat at the Belevedere with their feet on a chair and wouldn't pay a cent for their meals. Milton had to ignore them. He didn't want his cafeteria wrecked.

And then the Cannibals abandoned the Belevedere. That was Webster Avenue's last trace in our territory. The gang was gone. The cafeteria had become my summer hangout. I sat at the Wolves' old table with my sketchbook. Whatever talent I lacked, I still loved to sketch faces.

Percival sat down next to me. He had bandages on his knuckles from his last fight.

"You won, kid."

"How did I win, Percy? I met with Fitz for five minutes and he didn't even know who the Cannibals were."

"Well, it seeped down," Percival said. "I wouldn't count on it too much. The cops remember what they want to remember and forget everything else. We'll be back. But I have a proposition for you, kid. Why don't you fold the remains of your gang into Webster Avenue? That way we'll be twice as strong."

Percival was a fierce negotiator, fierce as his fists.

"No, thanks, Percy. I think we'll stay where we are."

He laughed. "Stay where you are? The Wolves don't exist. I haven't seen a jacket with yellow eyes in months—a year, maybe."

"What about mine?" I asked him.

"You don't count. You're a general without an army. With

Michael around it might have been different. Join us. You'll be your own master of a domain within a domain."

"No thanks."

And he left. But we were as vulnerable as ever. Another gang might step in. I had to gather the remnants of the Silver Wolves. I must have climbed a hundred flights of stairs. Half the Wolverines had gone over to the Cannibals and stayed with them. But I had to convince the other half. I worked on the clubhouse every afternoon for a week after I got back from M & A. I worked alone. I had to repaint the walls, get rid of the white skulls.

I went to Wallenstein. "Mr. W, you can't deal with the Cannibals anymore. This is our turf."

"But I'm a businessman."

"Then move to Webster Avenue," I said. "Southern Boulevard is out of bounds. And I'll

need more jerseys and jackets. Make the yellow eyes more prominent."

He cackled. "Jonah, there's already room for nothing else on the back but those yellow eyes."

"I don't care. I want them to stun and hypnotize whoever looks."

He cackled again as he set the table with digestive biscuits and a pot of Earl Grey with his tea cozy.

"What a sharpster you've become. You could pick my pockets while we're sitting here and I wouldn't even notice."

We drank the tea and I let the biscuits crumble in my mouth.

I HAD A HARD time assembling the gang. There wasn't much of a gang to assemble. Most of the members had gone on to other pursuits. I kept the clubhouse. It was vacant most hours.

But I was stunned. Housewives would stop me in the street, coming from the market.

"Bless, you, Jonah. It was a nightmare with those chalk faces around."

Shopkeepers waved from their windows. I made sure to wear my jacket with the enormous yellow eyes. A patrol car stopped while I was walking on Boston Road. A familiar voice sang out from the back seat.

"Get in."

I sat down next to Captain Shelly. He was wearing his uniform with the gold braids.

"Quite a performance, kid. Or should I call you General Jonah?"

"Cap, I'm not sure I have a single follower."

"Makes no difference. You impressed Fitz."

"Cap, he didn't even know I was alive."

"But you still managed to enlighten him," the captain said. "He visited Boston Road with his deputies, didn't he?"

"I thought it was a mirage."

The captain shook his head. "Mirage? I was there, kid. Fitz took it all in. And he liked what you wrote in your school paper, comparing him to Teddy Roosevelt. Fitz has his vanities. But I didn't suffer. He said, 'Shelly, I'm counting on you. Get those skulls back to Webster Avenue, where they belong. I'd rather have them there than at Rikers.' I got a merit badge and commendations, thanks to you."

"Then what do I owe you, Cap?"

"Your life," he said. "The Wolves still have to patrol the streets."

I looked into his vacant eyes. "I'm the only one of the Wolves that's still on his feet."

"Fine," The Cap said. "But keep wearing your jacket. I like the yellow eyes. They scare people away."

"You're not scared," I said.

"Me? I'm scared to death. Now get out of the car. I shouldn't be seen with the lord of the Silver Wolves. People might think you're my snitch."

My great mentor shoved me out of the car.

I walked to the Jennings Street market. Shoppers kept staring at me. Jake pranced away from his barrels and kissed me on the cheek. His apron was wet with brine. There was brine on his lips.

"Our savior," he said. "You will have a feast of pickles every single Sunday."

I shrugged my shoulders. "Jake, I didn't do all that much."

"Big talker," he said. "You got rid of the barbarians."

I went into the Russian bakery. It turned silent. Customers stood very still. The cashier, the counter girls, and the baker himself came out from behind the glass to clutch at my hand. They stuffed a shopping bag with honey cake, marble cake, sponge cake, coffee cake, cinnamon buns, and charlotte russes.

"For your mama," the baker said. "May she live to be a hundred."

"No," the cashier said, wagging her finger at the baker. "A hundred and five."

That was my life in the South Bronx. Alvin James held out a red bandanna in place of a white flag, and we met on Wilkins Avenue, the borderline between his visible gang, the Boston Road Barons, and my invisible one.

He smiled and we bumped elbows, a sign of friendship that I picked up from him at Spofford.

"How are you, juvie?"

"Surviving," I said.

"I wanted you to know that your turf is sacred ground."

I laughed. "What's so sacred? You're looking at the one and only member of the Silver Wolves."

"Ain't no matter," he said. "Fitz is on your side. No gang is gonna mess with you."

And he ran across the border line with that red bandanna, like a Black cowboy from Boston Road.

IT HAD NOTHING to do with bribes. Mr. Swann came out of his drugstore to give me a "donation" of five dollars. I wouldn't take ten from him. But I did take ten from Miller, the sporting goods man, who denied me my Willie Mays. Most of the stores in the neighborhood contributed to the Silver Wolves Welfare Fund. I was only doing the work that Michael had started. I scoured the neighborhood for the old and the lame. Landlords were reluctant to raise the rent of a sick old lady on Minford Place after the yellow eyes on my jacket stared back at them. Those yellow eyes were a wonder.

I didn't have to plead. I had the grocer on Seabury Place send his delivery boy to the old man with bronchitis in the basement apartment on Minford Place. Dr. Kulack, who was born in Odessa, and served the entire neighborhood, made a house call. He always chided me and Michael for lifting weights.

"It will make your heart big. Jonah Salt, your heart is also a muscle."

That didn't stop me from lifting weights. He treated the old man but wouldn't accept a penny. Kulack was the last angel we had on earth. He had wiry white hair and rimless spectacles. He talked about a writer from Odessa, Isaac Babel, who invented a gangster in orange pants, Benya Krik, and dwelled in a poor district called the Moldavanka, Odessa's equivalent of the South Bronx, where Jewish beggars and Jewish merchants lived side by side.

"Benya," he said, "where's your orange pants?"

"Dr. Kulack, I'm not Benya Krik."

"And what about that brother of yours? So smart and so dumb. He could have been a scientist. And what is he now? A captive at Castle Billy. He had bronchitis, too. Did you know that I visited him there? I rode the ferry, which was like jumping across a creek. And you? Are you into social work?"

"No, Dr. Kulack. But this is still Michael's domain. And I have to look after those who can't look after themselves."

"Then we're brothers, Benya." Half his patients he never charged. He was right out of the Moldavanka.

I walked him down five flights, carrying his medical bag, which was heavier than a 10-pound dumbbell. The neighborhood could never have survived without this white-haired doctor. His wife always screamed at him. She was his bill collector.

He knew me since I was a baby boy. He loved us. There couldn't have been many doctors like him. He worked seven days a week, visited patients in the middle of a snowstorm. Maybe he was a secret member of the Silver Wolves.

THE BEAUTY OF it all was that my sweetheart could return to the South Bronx. Merle was amazed. It confused her, mixed her up, that everyone was suddenly so nice to her. People stopped her in the street and kissed her hand.

"Jonah, what the hell is going on? I'm not exactly a movie star."

I boasted when I shouldn't have. "You are a movie star. You're with me. Haven't you noticed? Every damn chalk face is gone. And there are no more white skulls on the windows."

"And that's because you outsmarted the Police Commissioner?"

"Not at all. I just made him notice me."

We went to the Belevedere. Milton wouldn't allow me to pay the bill. I introduced Merle to the Widow, Rosalind Silverstein.

"Darling," she said, squeezing Merle's hand in camaraderie, "you're too good for this gangster."

"But he's *my* gangster," Merle said. And both of them laughed.

"Don't forget," said the Widow, as we were about to leave the Belevedere. "You owe me two sketches."

I pointed at her. "And you owe twenty dollars to the Silver Wolves Welfare Fund."

"Blackmailer," she said, "what do I care about your mission to save sick people?" And she gave me fifty bucks, which I noted in my little account book held together with a rubber band.

We went to Indian Lake. The boathouse wasn't under siege. The attendant had a hook that attached our rowboat to the lake's tiny wooden pier. Merle and I sat in the rowboat. I put the oars into the metal sockets and rowed away from the pier.

"My God," she said. "It's just like Venice. You're my gondolier."

"Merle, I've never been to Venice."

"Jonah," she said, "you've never been anywhere except to Convent Avenue and Castle Billy."

"That's not true. Didn't we go swimming in the Catskills? I have all those frogs to remember."

She began to sulk. "You know what I mean. Couldn't you come to Europe with us this summer?"

David had booked passage for the Messengers on the *Queen Mary*. He meant to tour the vineyards of Italy and France and then stop at his secret paradise of Gijón. He could have flown on the Pan Am Clipper, but he and Merle loved to watch the sea rip from the deck of an ocean liner.

"Your mom wouldn't have to be alone. Dad would gladly pay for her passage. Doesn't she ever go on vacation?"

Mom wouldn't have gone. She'd have considered it charity. And Amazing Milk Chocolate didn't believe in vacations for its employees. Mom was a piece worker, paid for the hours she stood at her station. And I couldn't let her come home to an empty house. It was the only time we had together, late at night. And I had other responsibilities.

"It isn't only that," I said. "I have to protect the neighborhood from scavengers. And the landlords are much nicer when I'm around."

I rowed across the lake. Families in other rowboats waved to us. I couldn't wave back, not while I was clutching the oars.

"Then will you be the guardian of Minford Place for the rest of your life?"

I didn't have an easy answer for Merle. "Don't you think I'd like to visit that magic town of your father's, that town off the calendar of time, where entire families go for a long ramble after dinner?"

"Then come with us, Jonah. Dad will hire a whole team of watchmen to watch your streets." She sat in silence, held a conversation with herself, and ended it with a smile. "I'm such a brat. Forgive me, Jonah. I'm just a girl who will be lonely without you all summer."

"There's nothing to forgive."

I kept listening to the splash of the water against the wooden blades and the squeak of the metal sockets with each stroke of the oars. It was like the sound of a baby crying.

TWENTY-THREE

The Tall Package

DAVID HELD A Bon Voyage party in the Messengers' stateroom on the morning of the *Queen Mary*'s departure. Many of David's associates and friends had come. He hired the caterers himself. I wasn't in the mood to eat, but I did taste a tiny frankfurter attached to a toothpick. I was amazed by the size of the ship. It was as wide as the Jennings Street market, higher than Hermann Ridder, and as long as two city blocks. Merle didn't invite her old friends from Music and Art, not even her brother and sister cubs on *Overtone*. She had broken with her past, except for the juvie with the toothpick. She served as a hostess, welcoming guests, but her smile was hollow.

"Kidnap me, Jonah. Carry me off this ship. Hide me in your cellar."

David called me over after he noticed the odd dazzle in her eyes. She could have been aboard another *Queen Mary*, a moon-girl on her own ocean voyage.

"Wait here," he said. "Don't move." He stood in the middle of the stateroom, with its plush carpets, leather couches, and soft lights, half hidden in the walls.

"Out," he said. "The party's over."

His guests looked at him in shock.

"Out, I said. Out."

They gathered their belongings and left. I'd never seen that hardness in David, the leader of a gang long gone. He wouldn't allow Alice and Flora to sit. I felt as if I was in the middle of a trial.

"Jonah," he said, "I'll have you hung by your big ears if you hurt my little girl."

I could have been back at Spofford. David had the grim grey eyes of a jailor.

"How have I hurt her?"

"She's in love with you, dammit, and she doesn't want to leave without you. The *Queen Mary* means nothing to her. The vineyards won't amuse Merle. Nothing will. Will you write her every day?"

"I'll try," I said.

"That's not good enough."

Alice intervened. "David, you're torturing the boy."

"Exactly," David said in a language I understood. He was still a gang leader, even if his gang had evaporated years ago.

"I'll write her every damn day," I said.

Merle wheeled right up to him. "Dad, he's not your servant. I don't want letters written on command."

"Merle, stay out of it. This is between me and . . . your suitor," David said.

"Dad, I'm sixteen. Jonah's my future and my best friend. And I'll kill him if he doesn't write me every day."

I WAS LONELY as hell without Merle and the Messengers. I couldn't send a letter to the *Queen Mary*. It didn't have a permanent address on the Atlantic. And then a boy in a blue uniform with a funny hat knocked on our door at Minford Place. He had a radiogram in his hand from the *Queen Mary*. I was so surprised by his visit that I tipped him a dollar. It wasn't easy to open the envelope, that's how tightly it was sealed.

> dear mr. editor-in-chief,
>
> i've been seasick from the moment we left port.
> the wind nearly blew me off the deck.
> i've retired to our cabin for the rest of the voyage.
> i've been so whoozy that i haven't had the time to miss you.
> i miss you now.
> love from mom and dad and flora and me
> your former cubby,
>
> merle

I was less lonely now, clutching that yellow radiogram with its block letters. I went down to the Figaro. It was a ghost café. The high schoolers were gone. There was no academic pressure in late June and July. I had a coffee with a snowcap. Then I walked along Bleecker. There was no street parade, no Carnival, no cluster of students. It was lonelier here than it was in the Bronx.

I rode the ferry to Governors Island. The captain blew his whistle the moment I came aboard. "Haven't seen you in a long time, son."

"Been busy," I said. But the captain couldn't hear a word through the blast of the whistle. The military police on board were as pugnacious as ever. They considered the circular prison on Governors Island their property.

I had my usual long sit at Castle Billy until Michael arrived. He was scrawnier than I'd ever seen. I felt as if I'd robbed him of his muscles and his flesh, grown bigger at his expense.

"You had bronchitis."

He stared at me. "Who told you that?"

"Dr. Kulack."

"Yeah, the bastards let him examine me. They couldn't figure out my cough. He brought me a vaporizer, the kind we had when we were little kids. The cough went away in a week. He says you sent the Cannibals running back to Webster Avenue. Jonah, you're our general now."

"Mikey, the Wolves are gone."

"It doesn't matter, kid. You've been getting medicine and food to sick people. That's what counts. It means we still have our turf."

That's all my brother had, the remembrance of a gang he started when he was eleven, when he scrubbed the dirt off a wounded wolf. The past was the only future he'd ever have. He'd turn into a boy with more and more missing teeth the older he got.

The guards took him away. I started my long trip back to the Bronx. I had a late dinner with Mom. She stopped bringing her notebook to the chocolate factory. That flash of words was gone from her head. It hurt too much to know that my brother would be stuck in a living grave for the rest of his life. I tried to console her.

"Anita, I'll become a lawyer. I'll go to Cornell. I'll find a way to get Michael out of Castle Billy."

Mom had a sad smile. "My big shot. You can't save Michael. No one can."

I brushed my teeth. I got into my pajamas and went to bed. I had the heebie-jeebies. I couldn't sleep. And then I dreamt of Michael's silver wolf. Mr. Merriman always said that a dream was the sign of something, but that something was never clear. I was walking with the wolf on a leash. We were at Indian Lake. Everyone stared at the wolf's yellow eyes.

"What an extraordinary pet," one of the strollers said.

"She's not my pet. She came out of the wild to visit me."

"What's her name?" another stroller asked.

"She doesn't have a name."

There was a gang in the park with chalk on their faces. But these weren't Cannibals. It was another gang, a gang I had never seen before. I wasn't sure what territorial rights they had, since Crotona Park was neutral ground. Still, they seized the park attendant's hook, latched onto rowboats, and returned them to the pier. They knocked off the attendant's cap and tossed it into the lake. Then they saw the wolf.

"Look what we have here," the leader of this rebel gang said. "A wolf on a leash—tame as a kitten."

They wanted to steal her from me. But the wolf broke away from the leash, leapt into the air like a silver comet, knocked the gang leader down with a bump of her body, and tore

into the shirts of the other gang members with her long teeth. These rebels ran from the park. Then the silver wolf returned to me. That's when I woke up.

Two days passed. I didn't get another radiogram from

Merle. I panicked, thought that the sea had washed Merle overboard. Then the boy in the blue uniform knocked on my door again. He handed me another radiogram. I had a rough time ripping the envelope open.

> *dear mr. editor-in-chief,*
>
> *call me captain couragious.*
> *i've left the cabin after two days of dizzy speels.*
> *dad has a surprise for you.*
> *he's been working on it for a year and a half.*
> *you should receive a package very soon,*
> *a tall package.*
> *even my chariot misses you.*
>
> *merle*

The *Queen Mary* still didn't have an address, and I couldn't write Merle at sea and ask her about the surprise package. The mailman usually arrived every morning at eleven, but he didn't have any packages for Mom or me. I waited near the mailbox for another two mornings, and then I gave up. I didn't like surprises.

I did my usual rounds. I sat with Dr. Kulack. His outer office was filled with penniless patients. His wife frowned at them and frowned at us. She was a relentless bookkeeper.

He scolded her. "Sonya, you'll embarrass me in front of the boy. He's become my biggest helper." He handed me a dozen prescriptions that I was supposed to deliver to the druggist, Mr. Swann. They were for patients who had every sort of illness, including old age.

"How's Michael?" he asked.

"His bronchitis cleared, thanks to you and your vaporizer." I stole glances at Sonya, who seemed to soften at this. Her hard gaze was replaced with something close to curiosity and compassion.

Dr. Kulack promised to visit Michael next month.

"Let me pay you, Doctor."

"Absolutely not," he said, glaring at his wife. "This boy is a godsend."

"He's a gangster," Sonya Kulack said, then shrugged. "Him and his brother. But he's also a blessing. My husband doesn't have to work so hard."

I brought the prescriptions to Swann, waited until he filled them, and then I ran up and down the stairs of a dozen buildings, delivering each prescription. One man in his eighties, Mr. Yarbrough, saw the yellow eyes on the back of my jacket, and said, "You're the Devil. I wouldn't take medicine from you."

I fed him his cough syrup and he quieted down. I realized soon enough that it was easier to deliver medicine by way of the roofs. It took me five hours. I was so exhausted, I took a nap in the middle of the afternoon. I never napped.

There was a pounding on our door, the smash of a fist. No one ever bothered to ring the bell.

"Come in," I said. The door wasn't locked. The banging grew louder.

"Hold your horses, whoever you are."

I opened the door. Two military policemen were standing in front of me with their armbands and their holsters. Between them was my brother, the tall package that didn't come through the mail. He was wearing a military overcoat, with his prisoner's pajamas underneath.

Castle Billy didn't even allow him the gift of shoes and socks. He'd come to the Bronx in his bare feet. The commandant wanted to humiliate Michael as best he could. My brother was half asleep. He tottered on his toes.

One of the MPs handed me a clipboard and a ballpoint pen. "Are you a relative of Claimant 497, formerly Private First Class Michael Salt?"

"Yes, I am."

"Sign here," said the second MP.

I signed a document I hadn't even read. And I had no authority to sign it. I wasn't eighteen. But the MPs didn't give a damn.

"Private First Class Michael Salt," said the second MP, "has been stripped of his rank and all his privileges. He's a civilian now."

The two cops from Castle Billy saluted me and left with the clipboard. David's "package" fell into my arms. I carried him into the apartment in his pajamas and military coat. He couldn't have weighed more than a hundred and twenty pounds. His lips were very dry and had sores on them. Michael's old bed sat there without sheets and pillowcases. It was Mom's way of mourning his absence. So I propped Michael down on my bed. I made him drink a glass of water and then I called Dr. Kulack. I left a message for Mom at Amazing Milk Chocolate, but I knew it wouldn't be delivered to her before her next coffee break.

Michael opened one eye, grabbed my hand, and said, "Where am I, kid?"

"At home, Mikey. On Minford Place."

He coughed twice and said, "That's a relief. I thought they were accompanying me to a firing squad."

I made him drink a glass of milk.

Kulack arrived. "A miracle," he said. He plucked off Michael's pajama top, listened to his heartbeat, tapped him on the back several times with his index finger, opened his medical bag, gave Michael a vitamin shot, smeared some salve on his lips, and said, "Jonah, feed him very small portions. His stomach has shrunk. He's undernourished and anemic. Give him plenty of vegetables and fruit from Jennings Street. I'll be back tomorrow."

I cut up an apple and a banana, put them in a bowl of Cheerios, added a clump of raisins, and some walnuts that I had to crack open with Mom's nutcracker, poured in some milk, took a spoon from the counter, and returned to Michael. I fed him like a baby when the telephone rang.

It was the captain of the *Queen Mary* on his radio phone. He introduced himself and put David on the line.

"Jonah, did the package come?"

"How the hell did you do it?"

I could hear him laugh. "I'm not even sure. Communiqués were sent from department to department. Some were never read. I hired a lawyer who'd once been attached to the military courts. He got through the maze. It seems Michael's commanding officer amended his statement, said he'd been drunk at the time, made some embarrassing remarks, and a file was opened. After being shoved back and forth it finally got to the Inspector General's Office. And then my own man could pounce and make his plea. Michael's sentence was rescinded. He didn't get an honorable discharge, but he's been 'separated' from the government and returned to civilian status. How are you, kid? I can't hog the captain's phone. What should I tell Merle?"

"Tell her—tell her that I love her radiograms. And—"

But I lost the line. Maybe there was a storm in the Atlantic. I went back to feeding Michael when Mom came into the room. She must have gotten my message at Amazing Milk Chocolate and ran all the way from the factory on Southern Boulevard. I'd never seen the look she had on her face—it was somewhere between devastation and bliss. Michael's skin and bones must have frightened her.

She clutched my arm. "Jonah, am I dreaming?"

"Yeah, Anita. We're all in the middle of a long, long dream."

THE CARNIVAL HAD moved to Minford Place. People stood outside our tenement waiting for Michael to appear. My brother had returned from the dead. The Cheerios and apple slices must have revived him. He didn't look so gaunt in sunglasses, a New York Giants baseball cap, and the gang's blazer. I saw a number of jerseys and jackets with yellow eyes in that crowd. Michael's release had restored the Silver Wolves. Even Dr. Kulack and his wife had come to greet our toothless general.

I heard a police siren. People had to make way for Captain Shelly's sedan. Shelly was planning to take Michael to see Pop at Creedmoor. There wasn't much point in my going along. I would have gotten in the way. And Mom didn't want to ride in the same car with Captain Shelly. She could see Pop another time.

There were children on the rooftops. The candyman had come from Crotona Park to hawk his jelly apples and bags of salted nuts. The Bungalow Bar boy couldn't get through the crowd in his ice cream truck. But another boy arrived with a freezer attached to his tricycle, and he sold popsicles and creamsicles before the ice cream truck could penetrate the crowd.

Michael was a war hero and he'd never been to war. Neighbors wanted to see the castaway from Castle Billy. Percival was in the crowd. He didn't need a white flag or a red bandanna. He'd come to welcome Michael. News of his return had reached the Belevedere. Members of the sewing circle and the chess club wanted to have a look at the Bronx's lost son. Rosalind Silverstein showed up with her bookkeeper and her bodyguard.

And then Michael stepped out onto Minford Place with the wolf's yellow eyes on his back. A touch of color had returned to his face. Mom stepped out after him. She was radiant. The little webs under her eyes had disappeared. The sadness that had overwhelmed her while Michael was condemned to Castle Billy was gone. She walked with the grace of a silver wolf.

Michael got into the police sedan. Children climbed onto the running boards and remained there while Shelly's driver wove through the crowd. The children jumped off when the sedan reached the end of the block. I stood with Mom in a drizzle of sunlight. We held each other as if our lives depended on it. Maybe it did.

Award-winning writer of noir **JEROME CHARYN** is the author of more than fifty published works, spanning novels, memoirs, graphic novels, short stories, plays, and creative nonfiction. His novel *Blue Eyes* (1975) inaugurated the widely popular and acclaimed Isaac Sidel series. His memoirs, *The Dark Lady from Belorusse* (1997) and *The Black Swan* (2000), were each named a *New York Times* Book of the Year. Charyn was also awarded a 1983 John Simon Guggenheim Memorial Fellowship in Fiction and a Rosenthal Award from the American Academy of Arts and Letters. A finalist for the PEN/Faulkner Award for Fiction, Charyn has also been named Commander of Arts and Letters (Ordre des Arts et des Lettres) by the French Minister of Culture. *Silver Wolves*, which closely mirrors his own teenage years in New York City, is his first young adult novel.